The Franklin Family Odyssey

HOMESTEADING IN ALASKA

The Beginnings

The Franklin Family Odyssey

The Franklin Family Odyssey

Copyright 2017 by David Erickson

The Franklin Family Odyssey

The Franklin Family Odyssey

Dedication

I would like to dedicate this book to the ministry team at C5 Church in Carson City, Nevada. What a team.

The Franklin Family Odyssey

The Franklin Family

Odyssey

HOMESTEADING IN ALASKA

The Beginnings

By David Erickson

The Franklin Family Odyssey

The Franklin Family Odyssey

Contents

DEDICATION..5

CHAPTER ONE..11

THE DREAM..11

CHAPTER TWO..25

THE FAMILY..25

CHAPTER THREE..47

THE STAKING..47

CHAPTER FOUR..75

THE CABIN..75

CHAPTER FIVE..93

THE SPRING, SHORT SUMMER AND NEXT LONG WINTER..93

CHAPTER SIX..104

MOVING IN AND THE BABY......................................104

The Franklin Family Odyssey

CHAPTER SEVEN 119

THE REUNION 120

CHAPTER EIGHT 136

THE DEADLY HUNT AND THE EARLY BUT EASY WINTER
.... 136

CHAPTER NINE 152

THE NASTY BREAKUP 152

CHAPTER TEN 168

THE FIRE 168

CHAPTER ELEVEN 178

THE MIRACLE 178

chapter one

the dream

Johnny Fergie Franklin was born in Northern California in a deep dark forest hundreds of miles from the nearest big city. His father and mother, John and Alice, were married just a year earlier in a large city near Los Angeles, California and immediately the couple moved north to get away from the big cities.

The local traveling doctor, who did house calls, had recently visited the Franklin's little cabin and told Alice, "My, dear lady, I may not make it back out here before this baby comes. Are you going to be alright? Can your husband assist you if the baby decides to come before I get back?"

Alice told the doctor, "We should be able

The Franklin Family Odyssey

to handle it. I helped my mom with my siblings. John will be a good help, thank you."

It was early September and John Franklin had prepared the firewood for the winter, repaired the cabin roof and was hunting for meat for the next six months. It was about that time that Alice told her husband that she was ready to have the baby. He just about had a heart attack.

While his wife labored in their large feather bed, John heated water and prepared to assist Alice as she attempted to give him birth instructions in the midst of going through her own labor pains. Baby Johnny was born that night and big John was the first to hold the little newborn. John washed up Johnny and wrapped him warmly in a blanket that had been knitted by Alice in the previous summer.

Within a few hours, the Franklin household realized a whole world of change.

The Franklin Family Odyssey

The mother and father were tending to a little baby's needs hourly in the daytime and at least every three hours at night. Big John found himself falling asleep while hunting and running out of energy while chopping wood.

Little Johnny grew quickly and within a short couple of years he was helping his dad with the chores. The youngster was two when he decided that he would help his dad haul the wood in from the outside.

One day Johnny followed his dad outside to the wood cutting area. The youngest Franklin got down on his knees and carefully grabbed a single split piece of wood. He held it close to his tiny chest. Then he got up slowly, and followed his dad through the doorway into the house. When he found the pile of firewood near the stove, he dropped the log out of his arms and it landed right on his own right foot. Needless to say, Little

The Franklin Family Odyssey

Johnny cried for hours and couldn't walk very well for some time.

Mom and Dad Franklin soon had twin boys, Denny and Donald, that came along three years after their oldest. Johnny, the name his parents called him, was an awesome older brother. He became the protector of his twin brothers who were born when he was three.

Before he turned five, Big John had Johnny hunting rabbits with a Remington 22 and fishing for the big one down at the little lake nearby. The oldest Franklin child was thrilled to be a part of his dad's everyday routine. Little Johnny was at dad's side of the bed at six AM almost every morning waiting to ask his daddy, "What we doing today, Daddy?"

When Johnny was five, it began. Almost every night the youngster had the same dream. It wasn't a really bad dream or a

The Franklin Family Odyssey

nightmare, but at times his recollection of the dream caused him some fear.

The oldest son would wake up in the middle of the vision and would be out of breath. Johnny would immediately sit up in his bed, and literally feel that he was in the midst of the activity that he had been dreaming about.

The young Franklin's dreams were persistent but he didn't share them with his parents for a few years.

As a little tyke, Little John was always very ambitious and he loved adventures. When Johnny was nearly eight and the twins were five, his dad decided he would take the three boys on a camping trip up into the southern Oregon Cascades about fifty miles from their home in California. The three boys were going with their dad on a real hunt for bigger game than they had seen in Northern

… California.

While they camped and hunted near Crater Lake, the three boys were supposed to learn from the elder Franklin, the art of camping and were also introduced to the skill of hunting to survive. Big John was hoping everything would run smoothly but what he did not understand at this point in his life, was that with three boys in the wilderness, for sure, there may be a few things that may not go as planned.

The twins were very hyper and high strung little guys that wanted to be in the middle of everything, especially in the middle of their food. The boys learned on this trip that they loved cooking hot dogs over an open fire. Big John thought that he had brought plenty of food for their little adventure in the woods, but the twins made sure they ate as much as they could and had a lot of it on their

The Franklin Family Odyssey

clothes every night.

One particular evening while big John was resting in the tent, Denny, the older twin, was very hungry and he found where his dad had stashed the hot dogs. While Donald watched, Denny grabbed two dogs, put them on a long stick, and proceeded to cook them over the open fire near the tent.

Within minutes the other twin, Donald, decided it was his turn to cook hot dogs so he attempted to take the cooking stick away from his twin brother. Seven-year-old Johnny watched the mêlée as Denny dragged his twin brother right into the fire. Big brother jumped into action and quickly pulled Donald out of the fire just before he set down down on a pile of hot coals. Denny dropped the stick in the fire and lost his hot dogs. He began to cry as he watched the dogs burn to a crisp in the flame.

The Franklin Family Odyssey

    John Franklin got up from his rest just in time to watch as Johnny brushed the hot ashes from Donald's sore backside. Little Denny was spotted leaning up against a tree crying and Donald was in shock. Needless to say, that evening everyone slept very well.

    Later, on the last afternoon of their hunting trip to Oregon, the boys had all been out tracking small game animals with their 22's. Franklin was teaching them all how to quietly stalk game. First, he would demonstrate while they were told to sit and watch from a distance. It was Johnny's job to keep the twins quiet and still.

    Johnny, himself, got really bored watching his dad and keeping track of his brothers. Within a few minutes, leaning up against a tree stump, he dozed off to sleep leaving his twin brothers to their vices which were many.

The Franklin Family Odyssey

Without anyone watching him, Donald immediately stood up and ran toward a big tree where he had heard some noise. Denny followed shortly thereafter. With their little rifles ready, quietly they stalked a prey like their dad had taught them. It was a small black and white animal that scampered into the woods.

A noise from the woods woke up Johnny and he found that his brothers were gone. Immediately he could smell a very strange and annoying odor floating in the air. The oldest son then heard voices several hundred feet through the trees so he ran as fast as he could to see if it was Denny and Donald.

The older brother watched as Big John carried a twin with each hand and walked precariously toward the nearby lake. He dropped them both in a shallow pool near the shore.

The Franklin Family Odyssey

That afternoon Johnny, as well as his twin brothers, realized that the skunk was an animal not to mess with. John spent the remainder of the day attempting to get the smell off of his twin boys while lecturing Johnny on responsibility.

When the boys returned to the cabin in northern California, Alice spent weeks soaking and cleaning the twin's clothes so they could wear them for at least one full winter. Johnny did what he could to help her and make up for his seven year old nap in the woods.

Little Johnny quickly grew to six foot before he was thirteen. Almost every week at least once, his regular dream would appear to him. One evening, after dreaming, he sat straight up in bed about midnight. He didn't know where he was. Johnny quickly jumped out of bed and hollered out, "Help!"

Big John heard his older son and

The Franklin Family Odyssey

hurriedly ran into the boys' room and grabbed Johnny and held him close.

Mr. Franklin whispered, "Johnny, what is it? Did you have a nightmare? Let's go to the front room and talk."

Johnny and his dad sat comfortably next to the wood stove. John lit a kerosene lamp and Johnny began, "This dream of mine...I've been having these dreams...I haven't told you or mom about them...cuz it didn't seem as important as cutting wood and taking care of the other kids."

Johnny continued, "Most of the dreams I have are very good. I mean they are adventures that I guess may happen to me. They are exciting...but this last dream.... everything happen and at the end....was very frightening."

Johnny stopped for a minute and

scratched his head, then he continued. "I go to a land far away from here. I think it's way up north somewhere. I guess they call it Alaska. Dad, do you know where that is? I learned of it in school."

John shook his head to affirm he knew of Alaska. "Is there more?"

The oldest son began again, "It was a warm night and we....There was a fire outside, I guess....Forest fire nearby.....We went to bed in a bedroom of the cabin and I think I remember a baby or young child. The fire caught the.... Dad, do I have to continue?"

"Son, will it help if you tell me or do you want to rest for a while?"

Johnny got up from his chair and continued, "I'll finish then I need to go for a walk. All this stuff is scaring me a little. I need to pray by myself out in the woods if that is

The Franklin Family Odyssey

OK."

"You don't have to finish if you'd like," Big John inserted.

"I'll finish. Not much left accept the fire. The cabin was on fire on the roof...That's what really scared me. I'm not sure if I, I mean we survived the fire. I woke up too soon. That's it, Dad."

Mr. Franklin stood up and pulled Johnny to his chest and prayed a quiet prayer with his oldest son.

As they finished the prayer, the twins ran into the living area and grabbed their Dad one on each side. Johnny released himself from the embrace and went outside.

John Franklin watched as his oldest son exited the cabin. He immediately knelt down and hugged his twins with a group hug, still thinking of his teenager, Johnny Franklin.

The Franklin Family Odyssey

chapter two
the family

It was a beautiful clear day in the Northern California back country. Johnny Franklin had prepared for this day for at least a year. His wife to be was at a cabin nearby dressing for the occasion.

Johnny paced back and forth in his parents little log house. His mom and dad were ready and sitting at their kitchen table made for five. The twins busied themselves together quietly in the corner near their tiered bunk beds. The younger boys were dressed in their best jeans and shirt and western tie for the special occasion.

Within an hour Johnny and Becka were joined in matrimony with the local pastor officiating. The reception party and dinner were filled with excitement as the local

The Franklin Family Odyssey

community showed up for the celebration.

The newlyweds moved into the little cabin Johnny and his dad had built the year before. The young couple loved their little house and daily worked on preparation for a northern California winter in a few months.

In early April while Johnny's wife rested in the cabin, the oldest Franklin son, as he had done frequently, walked over to his parents cabin which was located a couple of miles from his own.   He was in deep thought.

The young Franklin strolled slowly and stopped often just to contemplate his and Becka's future. Johnny was so distracted in his own thoughts that he almost walked right into his dad who was in the area chopping and collecting wood for the winter.

Big John called out, "Johnny, what's up? Are you sleep walking?"

The Franklin Family Odyssey

Johnny was startled when he heard his dad's voice. "Dad, what? Why? Sorry, I was thinking and not paying attention. I needed to talk to you. Do you have a few minutes or maybe longer?"

The older Franklin aimed the head of his ax into a partially cut log on the ground and then spoke, "Son, I always have time for you. You want to talk right here?"

Johnny walked up to a nearby tree, set on the ground next to it and then leaned back. He spoke, "Right here is great... Dad, I don't know what to do."

"What do you mean?....Are you unhappy with marriage already?"

"No, Dad it's not that. I'm very happy, and we have a great marriage, but...well, Becka's family is moving away. A long way from here."

The Franklin Family Odyssey

John set down next to his son on the ground near the tree then he spoke, "I guess you can't do anything about them moving...I knew they were thinking of moving to Alaska. He is hoping for a job up there and they want to stake a homestead."

"Dad, Becka wants us to move with them...to Alaska. I keep thinking about my dream…..Alaska?"

"Well, son, We've talked about this before, you are a grown man and I don't think you are a 'momma's boy.' You are a man of adventure and wouldn't you love the new surroundings? Don't let the dream determine your direction. Let God do that."

"Oh, yeh, it sounds incredible to have this new experience, but you and mom and my brothers are here in California. But...I've never been more than a mile away from you and mom in eighteen years."

The Franklin Family Odyssey

"Then what's the problem? You need to be out there on your own. Like I told you earlier... You are a man, now. So when will you guys leave?"

"Dad, I've really prayed about this and I'm sure we are supposed to go, but what about mom? How will she feel?"

"Your mom already knows, son. Like I said, I've known they were moving for months. And I knew you were going as well. She will miss you but she knows God will take care of you. She also knows about your dream. I had to tell her about it."

"Wow, I thought this would be harder. I'll come over and talk to mom tomorrow. We will leave in a month or so. It seems like it is too soon. I'm not sure if I'm prepared for this."

"Tell you what, Johnny, let's have a big

family gathering with you and Becka and her family before you head north. You are leaving in June?"

"The first of June, yes. The weather is better on the Alaska Highway through Canada in the late Spring. It may be raining and wet but not snowing a lot in June. That's what Becka's dad says."

John stood up and gathered the wood he'd been cutting and loaded a wagon parked nearby. The senior Franklin walked back toward Johnny who was still sitting near the tree.

Big John spoke, "Well it's settled. We will have a big family gathering around the first of June. I'll let you tell your mom, tomorrow, about you leaving and then she and I will put the plan in place. Let your wife know. We have over a month before we have to worry about missing you. Who knows, maybe we will be heading north as well."

"What? Do you mean that, dad?

"Well, I can't speak for mom, but I've been praying about it. I'm not ruling it out so help me pray."

"I'll do that dad. It would be really exciting if you and mom and the boys came north. I need to head home. Becka has probably got up from her nap by now. Can I bring Becka over tomorrow when I talk to mom? She hasn't seen her since Sunday."

"Sure, she would love it. Give me a hug and let me pray with you."

The father and son wrapped their arms around each other and big John prayed a short prayer of blessing for Johnny and his young family. The two went their separate ways as the sun poked its rays through the large trees of the Franklin Valley.

The Franklin Family Odyssey

Johnny hurried home to talk to Becka and let her know that he had his dad's approval as they approach this great adventure. The younger Franklin was also anxious to tell his wife that his parents may be coming to Alaska in the near future.

The Jones family and Johnny prepared for a few weeks for their long adventure through Canada and into the territory of Alaska. They attempted to anticipate and plan for anything that could go wrong or right on the two thousand mile trip into the frontier.

In early May, Mr. Jones and Johnny traveled to Los Angeles by train to purchase a brand new 1945 Chevrolet Truck and a sturdy trailer. They made sure the tires were of heavy duty construction and the truck had heavy shock absorbers for the rough Alaska Highway.

Young Johnny Franklin was given some

The Franklin Family Odyssey

quick lessons on automobile driving from Mr. Jones just before the two left for LA. The newlywed was then able to help with the driving on the return trip which took two days with camping out one night on the road. The younger Franklin decided he liked driving and now he was ready to help in driving on the two thousand mile trip north.

After the return from picking up the new truck, the two families had the big feast that John Franklin had planned a month earlier. The day before, John and Johnny had bagged a large buck which the ladies barbecued outside over a huge fire.

The twins felt the excitement and helped the ladies set up the big picnic table that the men had hauled in and placed near the Franklin cabin.

Just before sundown on June first the Jones and Franklin families set down to eat.

The Franklin Family Odyssey

They joined hands together and prayed a blessing on the food and protection for the long trip to Alaska that was scheduled for the following day.

When the dinner was completed, goodbyes were said to John, Alice and the twins. Johnny was the last one to head home to his cabin. He wanted to talk with his dad just one last time before the next day journey.

Johnny began, "Dad, you have taught me so much. I'm excited about helping the Jones' stake a homestead in Alaska. I'm anxious to help you stake one as well. When will you be leaving?"

"I don't know son. I'd love to come with you now but..probably before the fall. It will take a month and I still need my new truck."

"You are getting that soon, aren't you?"

"I plan on it, but I don't have all the

The Franklin Family Odyssey

money that Mr. Jones has. We have saved up some, but God knows and will have his own way. Son, we will be there by September. God has given me assurance."

"I'm very excited. Dad, I need a hug and then get home for some rest. Take care of my cabin until you leave. Maybe a newlywed family could use it."

"Your cabin will be used by someone.... Just get some rest...I'll see you in a few months."

The two Franklins embraced and parted their ways. Johnny ran toward his home to prepared for the next day's adventure. Halfway to his cabin, the young Franklin stop abruptly. He looked up into the sky, nodded his head in the affirmative, and raised his hands heavenward.

"Thank you, Jesus, for your assurance.

The Franklin Family Odyssey

Protect them and provide as they start north tomorrow. You have great things in store for Becka and I, and our families, but not my will only your will be done. Thank you, again."

The Jones' family and Johnny with Mr. Jones driving, left early the next morning on their long and rugged trip to Alaska. At first traveling rather slowly, two days later the family arrived near Seattle, Washington.

The highways in the US were paved and very passable. The weather was warm and dry.

With all their papers in hand Jack Jones planned on entering Canada by noon the next day. Just as planned they passed through customs a little after one PM.

Johnny rode as a passenger next to the passenger door while the two women squeezed between him and Mr. Jones. The young husband could not believe the beauty he was observing in southern British Columbia.

Canadian roads, outside of the big city of Vancouver became very rough. There were hundreds of miles of partially paved and unpaved roads on the route to Dawson Creek, BC where the actual ALCAN highway began.

Halfway to Dawson City near the community of Prince George, Mr. Jones asked Johnny if he was ready to take a turn at driving. Of course, he was anxious to take his opportunity at the wheel. About that time it started to rain.

Just outside of Price George the highway was dirt and because it was raining, the dirt road became a muddy mess. Before the family could get to Dawson Creek, Johnny had to slow way down because the road had become almost impassable. The truck began sliding all over the narrow road and the trailer nearly

The Franklin Family Odyssey

tipped over into the ditch on the right side of the highway. He finally brought the truck to stop.

Water ran like a river down the highway as they parked there on the edge of the muddy road. Johnny didn't know what to do.

Mr. Jones got out of the truck into the pouring rain. It was nearly dark. Johnny's father in law, with rubber boots on his feet, sloshed to the back of the truck and noticed the trailer had slid partially into the ditch. He called for Johnny.

The young Franklin heard Jack's voice, pulled his hat over his ears, and exited the pickup.

Johnny could see his father in law was attempting to push the trailer back onto the road. The young man quickly ran over to help him.

The Franklin Family Odyssey

A half hour later the two men were able to push the trailer back onto the muddy dirt road. Soaking wet they returned to the truck, this time with Mr. Jones driving.

After comfortably sitting behind the steering wheel of the pickup, Jack Jones spoke, "Johnny, you did really well with the truck and trailer, but you need a break from this storm. I'll find a place for us to stop for the night, my dear family. We need to dry out and let this storm pass over."

The family agreed.

A few minutes later they arrived in Dawson Creek and found a boarding house to wash up and spend the night. Mary Jones and Becka were very appreciative for the opportunity to bathe after a week on the road..

Johnny Franklin and Jack Jones were glad

to be in a dry place and needed to rest for a few hours. The family slept well that evening.

Early the next morning Johnny ventured outside to get some air. He was surprised to see six inches of snow on the ground in front of the boarding house. The young Franklin quickly returned to their room and dragged his wife outside to see the site.

Needless to say, the family was stuck in Dawson City for a few days, waiting for the unusual snow fall to melt and dry up before continuing on their journey north.

Johnny and Becka Franklin spent most of their down time touring Dawson City and sightseeing in the historical gold mining town. The young wife kept telling Johnny that this experience would be something incredible that they could share with their future children.

The Franklin Family Odyssey

Later that day the young Franklin wife informed her husband and family that she was pregnant.

The following night at the boarding house, Johnny's childhood dream returned again for the first time in months. At two in the morning he woke up in a start. Becka woke up, as well.

"Johnny, what's wrong. Did you have a nightmare?"

Johnny shook the cobwebs out of his head and answered, "I'm not sure it was a nightmare but my old dream is back. This time it really scared me. Can we pray together for this. I think the event in my dream is really going to happen and we need to be prepared."

The young couple held hands and Becka led them in prayer for the family, the future, and the trip to Alaska. She asked God to have

The Franklin Family Odyssey

his perfect will in the situations of Johnny's dream, and, "Dear, Lord, help us to be prepared for what might happen in our future. Thank you. Amen."

After two days of down time in the northern British Columbia city, the family fueled up their truck and several large metal gas cans. They were told by the locals that fuel stations were scarce in the stretch between Dawson City and Frazier Lake so the family would leave town prepared.

Another addition fact Jack Jones learned before leaving Dawson was that they needed protection from mosquitoes this time of year, especially in the Yukon. He purchased mosquito masks for his family which they would need to wear for protection if outside for a considerable period of time.

As they traveled deep into the interior the roads got worse and worse. In some

The Franklin Family Odyssey

places the mud was a foot deep but the weight of the pickup truck kept it on the sloppy road.

It took the family two days to get into the small village of Watson Lake in southern Yukon Territory. They found a fuel station and a place to take showers.

That evening they decided to set up their tent near the lake. Without thinking, they had forgotten to wear the mosquito mask that Jack had purchased and consequently while sleeping, they were tortured by the local insects.

Without the proper medication all four family members suffered from itchy skin that turned red and got infected. A day later, in Whitehorse, Yukon, they found some medication to ease their pain and inching. At that point the travelers made a decision not to neglect their protective mask the rest of the trip.

The Franklin Family Odyssey

Before leaving the capital city of Yukon Territory, Johnny checked the tires on the truck and the trailer. He noticed one of the rear tires on the pickup had a big tear on the inside and was losing air slowly. It was Friday evening and the tire store was getting ready to close.

Mr. Jones was told that the garage didn't have the right tire size for their truck. It would have to be ordered and wouldn't arrive until Monday, sometime. Jack ordered two tires and the family spent the weekend as tourist while they waited for the tires.

Monday morning early with Johnny driving, the family continued the journey north.

As they got closer to the Alaskan border the roads became extremely treacherous with steep climbs and long down hills stretches. The weather was dry but the roads slowed the

The Franklin Family Odyssey

vehicle down to less that twenty-five miles per hour.

Becka and her mom starting getting really car sick about the time they arrive near a large lake called Kluane, just northeast of Haines Junction. It was extremely hot that day so everyone went for a swim in the cool lake water.

That evening the Jones and Franklin families camped out close to the lake and celebrated the Fourth of July with their own picnic. Mr. Jones read from the Bible and they all thanked the Lord for a glorious day at Kluane.

After a good night's sleep Mr. Jones drove the pickup back onto the Alaska Highway and within a few hours they came into the small town of Beaver Creek which was 21 miles from the Alaskan Territorial border.

The Franklin Family Odyssey

Once crossing the Alaskan border, the roads, though still rather rough, were maintained better and Mr. Jones was able to drive much faster than the day before. The pickup pulled into Tok, Alaska later that evening.

The highway sign in Tok informed the family that Delta junction, the end of the Alaska Highway, was a little over one hundred miles away, and from there the family would drive north on the Richardson Highway another hundred miles to Fairbanks, Alaska.

With Johnny driving, the family arrived in Alaska's second largest city, a day and a half later. The skies were clear and the temperature was in the 80's. They quickly found a place to stay and Mr. Jones began checking into where they needed to go to get information on staking their homestead.

chapter three

the staking

Mr. and Mrs. Jones, Johnny Franklin and his young wife, Becka, stayed in Fairbanks in a boarding house for over a month while all the paper work for the homestead staking was processed. Jack Jones checked weekly on the progress of their application while working a few hours a day at his new job. Early in September after a beautiful Alaskan summer, Johnny and Jack picked up the completed forms and began planning their trip to the homestead area by Alaska Railroad.

In mid September the family of four traveled by steam engine railroad to a little place called Ferry, Alaska, a rail stop approximately one hundred miles south of Fairbanks. This stop was situated a mile south of Windy Creek Homestead Area in the interior of the Alaskan Territory.

Jack Jones had prearranged to rent a

The Franklin Family Odyssey

little log cabin near Ferry, which was on the Nenana River. The family would stay there in the one room cabin for a few weeks while they staked the forty acres that Mr. Jones had applied for.

Johnny could not believe the beauty that they beheld, as they walked up toward the homestead area, just a few miles from the little cabin. Birch and black spruce trees could be seen for miles in every direction.

As they climbed up to the plateau above Ferry, to the south they located the Alaska Range and the foothills that preceded them. Below their viewpoint and toward the west, the Nenana River wound its way through the deep valley northward toward the Yukon River.

Breathless and looking back toward his wife, Johnny commented, "What do you think, Becka? Isn't this incredible?"

Slowly reaching the ridge, Becka grabbed her dad's arm as he walked slowly into an open area. Then she spoke to Johnny, "I really haven't had time to look. I've been struggling just getting up here. I'll be OK."

Johnny quickly retorted, "You are tough lady, Becka. You can handle this. It is beautiful."

Becka walked slowly up to Johnny and hugged him from behind, then she softly spoke, "Yes, my dear, it is beautiful, but can we go back down to the cabin and rest for a while. I can help you and dad stake tomorrow. I would appreciate lying down for a few minutes."

Jack and Mary walked hand in hand for a few hundred yards down the trail that came across at the top of the hill. Jack looked back toward Johnny and Becka and said, "Tis a very beautiful place. Tomorrow the four of us will walk down this trail. The paper work says the homestead area begins a mile up this path. There will be a milepost. Let's head back to Mr. Devere's cabin and get some rest, and we will get started first thing tomorrow. We need to get going on this staking and cabin building before winter closes us down."

Mary spoke softly, "Yeh, and before the baby is born."

They all laughed and slowly headed back down the steep trail to Devere's Cabin near the railroad tracks.

The next morning, Johnny was up before the sun peaked into the deep valley of the Nenana River. He walked outside alone after putting a few logs on the wood stove to take the chill off.

The young Franklin walked down the tracks for a few minutes and then turned around. On his return back toward the cabin he notice Mr. Devere smoking a cigar out near the outhouse.

Devere called out, "Mr. Franklin, Johnny is it? Good morning."

Johnny was startled but quickly shook Devere's hand and began, "Yes, sir, Mr.

The Franklin Family Odyssey

Devere. I'm Johnny Franklin and the young lady is my wife, Becka. Sure is beautiful country."

"Yea, it's beautiful now, but next month the cold will come if not sooner." Devere puffed on his cigar and walked over closer to where Johnny stood near the tracks.

The old man continued, "You guys plan on building on your homestead this year? It could be tough this winter."

The young Franklin interrupted, "We...we plan on building as soon as possible. Our savings are running low staying in a boarding house in Fairbanks. My parents will be here in a few weeks to help us. We all have built cabins before. Not in the winter in Alaska but we can do it."

Just as Johnny finished his sentence, Jack walked out of the little cabin and strolled over to where Devere and Johnny stood.

Mr. Jones spoke, "Good morning Mr.

The Franklin Family Odyssey

Devere, son. Nice and crisp this morning."

Devere spoke, "Yeh, was telling your son in law, here, that this is nothing compared to the cold coming in a few weeks. You fellas are going to build this winter?"

Mr. Jones walked over to the railroad tracks and looked up the tracks to the north. Then he asked, "Can we get supplies up here on the train in the winter? Or should we hire a truck?"

The old trapper wandered over to where Jack stood and answered, "The train is expensive...but so is hiring a truck. I may have a friend in town, that is Anchorage, that can get the stuff to the other side of the river. Now, getting all that lumber up to your home site...not so sure."

"We will be taking trees from the property to build the cabin but we will need timber for the floors and interior walls. We could cut our own timber if we had a mill."

The Franklin Family Odyssey

Devere thought for a moment while pulling on his long beard. He answered, "Jones, you are a smart man. I can get you a mill instead if you have plenty of trees for your cabin. When will you stake your site?"

"We are going to get started today. All of us will walk back into the bush and hopefully choose the property this week. We are kind of picky, especially the ladies. Johnny and I have an idea what we are looking for. My son-in-law's parents will be arriving later this month. We are going to spy out a place for them, next to ours. We've been neighbors for many years."

Johnny interrupted, "We need to get those ladies ready to walk up, don't we, dad?"

"Yes, we'd better eat breakfast and get the wives ready. Devere, are there any horses around here for hauling up to the homestead?"

The old man quickly answered, "Naw, the miners don't use horses. Horses are very expensive to feed and they really are inefficient in the cold. The guys up at the mines leave vehicles over here near my cabin. I might be able to get them to loan one of them to you this winter. Two problems, though."

Johnny asked, "What problems?"

Devere quickly answered, "Can you get one of these vehicles started now and then start it every day during the cold winter. You guys think you could handle that?"

Johnny answered, "Mr. Jones, here, is a mechanic. But what do you mean about this winter?"

Jack inserted, "Gasoline powered vehicles don't start to easily in the cold. The oil thickens and the combustion is inhibited. In California we heated the block to start the heavy trucks we used."

"As I said before, you are a smart and informed man," Devere commented. "We use

The Franklin Family Odyssey

LP gas and a weed burner tool. The gas is good until minus forty. Then it won't flow."

"So we need a weed burner and some LP gas. Where do we get that stuff?" Johnny asked.

"They have the stuff all over Fairbanks. Guys, I have to run. When you want to start the tractor let me know. Talk to you gentlemen later."

Devere hurried back toward his cabin.

Johnny and Jack strolled back to the other cabin about a hundred feet away. Mary opened the door and announced, "Breakfast, guys. Are you ready to eat?"

The young Franklin hurried past his father-in-law and answered, "I'm ready and I'm sure dad is, too. What's for breakfast?"

Mary spoke, "Hot cakes and homemade syrup. Is that fine, Jack?"

Mr. Jones was contemplative and not

very talkative. He didn't answer right away.

Mary continued, "Jack, are you OK? Are you ready for hot cakes?"

Jack finally spoke, "I'm ready. Just thinking of all the things we need to do in the next few weeks. Johnny and I learned a whole lot from Devere this morning...about preparing, building and getting our supplies out here. Let's eat. We can talk about this later. We need to get staking."

An hour later the whole family was carefully walking in the thick forest when Jack Jones found the post that marked the beginning of the Windy Creek Homestead area. They followed a distinct trail.

Jack and Johnny carried long machetes strapped to their belts that would be used to cut brush if needed. Mr. Jones also brought a compass and carried a revolver on his hip.

Slowly the family followed the trail which wandered out of the trees and east through a shallow valley and then onto an almost treeless ridge. The trail continued north, with what Devere later called a muskeg bog, situated on the left.

The ladies walked together with their own conversation continuing on every step. Johnny followed directly behind Jack with very little talking. Franklin's eyes were constantly spying the country around him, while Mr. Jones was focused on the trail in front of him.

An hour into their hike, Johnny noticed a grove of evergreens mixed with a few short willows. He got Jack's attention and pointed. The group headed that direction.

Johnny was the first one to trek down into a shallow valley where a fast moving creek flowed. The family wandered toward the running water and Jack heard something that sounded like someone chopping wood on the ridge above them.

He called out, "Hello, is someone up there? "

The Franklin Family Odyssey

A white bearded gentleman walked out of the forest carrying an ax. He called back, "Hello there. You here to stake a homestead? By the way, I'm Mike Brooks. My girl friend and I just staked forty acres in the woods behind me. You might want to consider staking a half a mile north of here. It will border on ours."

Brooks pointed toward the east then he continued, "Our eastern boundary is across that creek and up that little hill. We brushed it a bit. You could probably walk through there pretty easily."

Jack thanked Brooks and directed his family toward a spot on the creek where they could cross. To make it easier for the ladies, Johnny and Jack found a few short logs to place across the stream. All four homesteaders crossed safely and continued down the trail that Mike had suggested.

As they walked up the little hill, Jack noticed the corner stake of Mike Brooks' forty acres. Seconds later Johnny pointed out to the family what looked like a spring of water coming straight out of the ground near the trail.

Within minutes the family spotted the north western stake of the Brooks' property, and Johnny ran ahead through an opening in the trees.

He called back to the other three, "Look at this! Trees all over this property. A beautiful place for a cabin right here in this small meadow. Dad, Becka, look at this!!"

Becka and Jack quickly found the young Franklin in the opening. Mary followed apprehensively.

Mary spoke, "Jack, is this where we are going to stake our homestead? How far did we walk, anyway. I'm afraid, my dear husband."

Jack turned around and looked back to his wife. Then he reached out his arms toward her and said, "My dear wife, God led us here.

Don't you believe that? It will be tough but we are tough. You are tougher than all of us here."

Mary looked down to the ground and covered her face with her hands. Jack embraced his wife and held her warmly.

While the Jones held each other, Becka grabbed her husband's hand and the couple walked around the property for over half an hour. Johnny and his wife dreamed of what could be done on their property.

Becka found a place for the garden and her husband pointed out trees that could be used for the cabin.

When the Franklins returned from their walk, the older couple was still talking. Becka skipped up to where her parents stood.

"Mom, Dad, we found a place for the garden, and Johnny found some great trees for the cabin."

Mary inserted, "We have to haul water

all the way from that spring back there. I'm not so sure you can take care of a baby up here in the middle of nowhere."

Becka commented, "But, Mom, you did with me..in the middle of the wilderness in Northern California."

Johnny interrupted, "Yeah, and my mom had me and the twins in the wilderness, sort of."

"Let's stop for a minute," Jack said sternly. "Let's give this whole thing to God. Mary has her concerns. You two have great ideas. I'm kind of in between. The Bible says that we should count the costs. We need His complete will for our family. Johnny's parents will be arriving any day now. My gut says to take the ladies back to town tomorrow. Then Johnny and I will come back out here and stay, at least until we get the boundaries brushed. That's our first requirement according to the territory authorities. We have a few hours, so today we should walk around and assess what we need as far as equipment. When Johnny

The Franklin Family Odyssey

and I come back we will be prepared to brush the boundaries quickly. Winter is coming."

The family finished the day's task and headed down to Ferry. They spent the night in the little cabin and woke up to a pouring down rain. The family packed up and caught the daily train back to Fairbanks.

It took Becka and her mother, a few days to recuperate from the trip to the homestead. Two days later the elder Franklins arrived in Fairbanks after a long hard trip from California.

It was the Sunday after Johnny's parents arrived that both families walked to a little church not far from their boarding house. The women especially enjoyed the lady minister who presented the Word that day. The twins told their family that they had made friends with some teenagers who were there. All eight decided they would love to return for services as often as possible.

Later in the week the three older gentlemen decided that they would take the

The Franklin Family Odyssey

train to Ferry and stay for a couple of weeks to get the staking done. Denny and Donald were to stay with the ladies. Everyone was concerned that the first cold or snow could come at any time since the temperatures at night were already freezing or below.

On Monday the three older males of the family purchased tickets and they arrived at their destination a couple hours before dark. Since it was officially moose hunting season in the territory, Jack decided earlier in the day, that they should bring their rifles along and do some hunting at the homestead area. Jack Jones had noticed plenty of sign that moose were in the area.

Johnny asked, "Jack, what will be do with the meat. It's not cold enough to store it outside and well, there are lots of predators looking for meat as well."

Mr. Franklin inserted, "I've heard of guys burying the meat in the permafrost in a deep hole if it can be dug. Let's get up there before dark and spy the area. Tomorrow we'll build a big fire and then dig a freezer in the tundra."

The threesome nodded agreement, packed up some gear and ammo, and started their trek of three miles back into the bush.

Jack took the lead carrying his revolver on his hip. As Big John hiked the tail, he watched for anything that moved. Johnny carried his 30-06 at the ready as it got darker.

The older Franklin handed the other two, miner lights he had purchased to help brighten their pathway. Johnny asked his dad how they operated.

John told him, "They light up with some kind of portable battery that was just invented a couple years ago. I hope they last at least a few days because I didn't grab any spare ones."

Johnny play with the light, turned it on then answered, "Pretty neat. It's bright. Let's look for a big moose."

Jack Jones looked around and said,

The Franklin Family Odyssey

"Hush, guys, do you hear that?"

Jones led the way as they crept in the direction that the sound had come from. A few steps later Jack put his hand back to stop the other two. He walked a few steps into the brush and motioned for the other two to come.

"It's nothing guys. just a little bear cub." Jack announced. "But...the momma bear is probably nearby. Let's head the other direction for now."

Darkness moved in, and the three men hiked the same trail to the homestead as the family had done in the previous week. The team walked past the Brook's property and down the boundary line toward what they hoped would be their future home site.

Earlier in the day, Jack had stuffed a three man tent into his pack. Each man brought a sleeping bag to spend at least one night in the bush. Johnny was anxious to start hunting for moose first thing in the morning.

The Franklin Family Odyssey

When they arrived in the clearing of their future home site, Johnny asked, "What's to eat?"

"You didn't bring anything," his dad asked. John handed his son a stick of jerky that he pulled out of his own backpack. "Next time, son, bring your own. Just kidding. Let's get some sleep and get up early tomorrow. There's bound to be a moose for us in this big country."

Jack was quiet as he prepared the tent and rolled out his bag. Johnny started a fire near the entrance to the tent, sat down and stared at the flames.

Big John noticed that Jack kept looking around into the dark woods that surrounded the team. Franklin walked over to his friend and whispered, "Something troubling you? You are very quiet. Is there a predator out there somewhere?"

Jack finally spoke, "A couple of things... My dear, Mary is apprehensive about moving

The Franklin Family Odyssey

up here into the middle of nowhere. But my biggest worry, right now, is the movement down below us...Maybe one hundred yards."

"Should we take a look, and make sure? This is the wilderness. The animals are in charge around here," John Franklin said softly.

Johnny stood up after hearing the conversation coming from behind him. Then he spoke, "Whats up? Are we going somewhere?"

Jack announce, "Your dad and I have to do some investigating. You keep the fire going. We will be right back."

The young Franklin contemplated as he walked back to the fire. He carefully put another log in the flame and then looked back as the two older men disappeared into the dark. He listened intently but he didn't hear a thing for a few minutes, but he grabbed his rifle for assurance just in case danger was near.

The Franklin Family Odyssey

Johnny jumped to his feet when he heard the noise of a gunshot coming from behind their camp. Carrying his 30-06, he ran to the edge of the meadow where his dad and Jack had disappeared a few minutes earlier.

A bright beam of light emanated from Johnny's head gear into the woods. At that moment he couldn't see anything but trees. Suddenly, he watched as Jack walked up the hill toward Johnny's position in the meadow.

Jack called to Johnny, "Grab your knife and your gun and follow me."

Quickly the young Franklin found is knife and caught up with Jack at the bottom of the little hill. The two men hurriedly headed east to where John awaited them.

Two hours later the three tired men hauled the final cuts of a young moose back into their camp in the meadow.

Later that evening while the others slept, Johnny took the first watch to protect their

The Franklin Family Odyssey

winter meat supply from predators. In turn John and Jack took a watch.

The three men were very tired when the sun cracked the horizon the next morning, but they had to keep moving because the team had a full day ahead of them.

The first thing the trio did was to hang the moose loins from a nearby tree limb in order to bleed the carcass. Then they prepared the ground to bury their bounty.

Jack had learned as he prepared to move to Alaska, that in the late summer months, the permafrost is melted, to a certain extent, to about a foot or two below the surface of the ground. There they would encounter frozen dirt or ice.

He also read that if the frozen ground was warmed by a blazing fire, then left to smolder, the permafrost would begin to melt gradually. The team needed to dig at least three feet deep to bury their meat.

The Franklin Family Odyssey

John asked his friend Jack, "How are we going to dig this stuff? We didn't bring a pit or a shovel, did we?"

Jack shook his head to say no and then spoke, "No, but I think I'll run down to Devere's and borrow a pick and shovel if he has one. You and Johnny keep the fire going and guard the meat. I'll hurry."

In a flash, Mr. Jones was gone. Johnny continued to stoke the fire at the location of the dig. Big John collected plenty of dead wood and piled it up near the blaze.

Before too long, lying next to the fire, Johnny fell asleep. Big John came back from the forest with an arm load of medium logs and he found his oldest son snoring.

The elder Franklin did not want to wake his son but someone needed to stay awake to protect their meat stash. John shook his son and he woke in a start.

"Sorry, Dad, I'm really tired. I will stay

awake from now on. Just keep making a lot of noise. That should do the trick."

"It's OK, son. We all are tired, but we need to be alert for a few more hours."

Big John turned around to walk back into the trees for another load of firewood and he heard a bit of noise coming from down the main trail that led into the home site. Johnny jumped up and ran down the winding path.

At a distance the young Franklin could see Jack stumbling toward them carry several tools. Johnny trotted out to meet Jack and grabbed a pick and shovel from his father-in-law, and they both walked back to camp.

Before the warm sun set that early fall day, the three men had the moose meat safely wrapped, buried and covered with dirt.

After eating a quick dinner, Johnny, his father and father-in-law crawled into their sleeping bags and fell fast asleep.

The next morning John was the first to

hear a noise coming from the nearby forest. Quickly he got up and woke Jack. The pair grabbed their rifles and swiftly scampered into the trees. After walking a few hundred yards they spotted a long fluffy tail disappear into a bush.

John quietly whispered, "It looks like a fox...but maybe something bigger is chasing it."

Jack answered, "Wait! To your right, John."

Within seconds the two friends were on the ground. They immediately spotted a mamma bear who lumbered through the woods in the direction of the little fox. A moment later the bear also disappeared into the brush.

Jack quipped, "I guess mamma must be busy right now. Let's head back to camp."

The twosome got up from the ground just as Johnny arrived. The young man was wondering what all the commotion was about out in the woods.

The three men walked casually back to the camp, they quickly fixed and ate their breakfast, and then began measuring the boundary that adjoined the Brooks' property.

The next three days Johnny and John measured and marked while Jack used one of the machetes to brush as much boundary line as he could. By the end of the second week, the team had completed this task and were preparing to pack their gear to head back to Fairbanks.

John began, "Well, let's get back up to the city and check on the pregnant lady and the other two women."

Jack inserted, "Yea they are probably thinking the wilderness gobbled us up. It'll be nice to sleep in a warm bed."

Johnny spoke, "I can't wait to tell the ladies about our meat stash. Hopefully they will be proud of us."

They all laughed and began their walk back to the Nenana River to catch the train to the city. The team had to wait a few hours once they arrived at Ferry. Their interest was piqued by the several stories Devere told them as they lingered.

Within a few hours Johnny and his brushing partners arrived at the boarding house and reunited with their wives and the twin Franklins. The men all took showers, cleaned up, and then they all went out to a nice restaurant not too far away.

That evening all the family members slept well, with dreams of cabin building in their dreams.

The Franklin Family Odyssey

chapter four

the cabin

On a crisp, late September morning with the Franklin twins leading the way, (not really knowing where they were going), the three families trekked closer to the staked out homestead near Windy Creek.

The hiking family arrived in the clearing near the northern brushed homestead boundary when Becka, full of excitement, asked, "Is this it, Dad? This is it?" Turning to her husband she continued, "Where will the cabin go again, Johnny?"

Johnny quickly responded, "Yes, this is our forty acres. Right here, my dear Becka. This is the best place for the cabin because it's already cleared. The rest of the property is covered with heavy forest or brush and some bogs filled with water. Just fifty feet east of where we stand is the hole we buried our winter meat supply in, if the bears haven't dug it up by now."

The Franklin Family Odyssey

Jack took Mary's hand and walked her in direction of the southern brushed line. They strolled a few hundred feet down the right away and the Franklin teenage twins spotted them, and quickly followed.

John noticed in the distance that his curious younger boys were following Jack and Mary down the path so he called to them, "Hey boys, Johnny and I want to show you some trees we will chop down this week. Come quickly."

Denny and Donald heard their dad's call, hurriedly turned around, and ran swiftly back to the clearing where their older brother stood waiting. For the next few minutes the foursome wandered through the forest picking out suitable trees for the first cabin to be built in the next few weeks.

Later Becka, her mom, and Alice found a comfortable place to sit and talked about family matters and babies.

Before the sun set in the southwestern

The Franklin Family Odyssey

sky, the large family decided to start their walk back to Devere's cabin at the river. Within an hour they were in view of the little log cabin.

Almost immediately after arriving and eating their dinner, the families were ready to call it a night. Everyone slept well their first night in their crowded little temporary home.

Early the next morning the men and teenagers, leaving Becka and the two older ladies at the little cabin, gathered the equipment they needed; some that they had borrowed from Devere. The men loaded the trailer that would be hauled up to the property behind Devere's tractor which was parked near the railroad tracks.

While Johnny Franklin's twin boys explored the area down near the Nenana River, John and Jack gassed up the tractor and attempted to start it up.

By the time Denny and Donald had

returned from their adventure, the tractor was spitting out black smoke and roaring loudly in the river valley. Within an hour the small group was climbing the hill to the trail, followed closely by the tractor and trailer driven by Mr. Jones.

An hour later the men and boys arrived at the property. The twins quickly found a way to get lost in the woods while the adults walked the land at length, marking suitable trees for log cabin construction. The men searched for tall and straight, white or black spruce trees that were at least eight inches in diameter at the bottom. Jack Jones wanted an eight foot wall so he figured they would need ten or eleven good size logs for the longer walls.

Jack studied a log cabin style he thought might work in the north, because of the use of the shorter spruce trees. The longest log with very little taper had to be sixteen feet long according to the plan he had penciled out. By lunch time the three men had picked out a dozen good sized trees and readied them for falling.

The first set of trees to be cut down had to have a wider diameter and approximately six foot long with very little taper. These were to be used for the footings that would be buried on the four corners and one on each side halfway between the corner posts.

The twins returned from their exploring and asked what was for lunch. John responded, "Alright boys, we didn't bring you two up here just to roam the woods and eat. After lunch we will need your help. We'll be chopping more trees after we have soup."

The identical Franklins looked at each other, nodded to their dad and sat down on a log near the fire where the broth was warming. The building crew, after being served by John, quickly ate the hearty soup that Mrs. Jones had prepared for them the night before. Everyone was satisfied and headed back into the forest to cut more large spruce trees which were about forty foot tall.

The Franklin Family Odyssey

    Denny and Donald were told to watch, at the beginning, so they could learn what had to be done on the next tree. Jack, after hauling the previous cut logs, had prepared the tractor by fitting the vehicle with a dragging cable hooked to the log once it was dropped. Johnny and John took turns with the ax.

    Later in the afternoon the twins were taught how to de-limb the trees on the ground with a sharp hatchet. They took turns with the hatchet until the team picked up another one when they returned to Fairbanks in two weeks.

    By nightfall the men and boys were totally ready to get a good night's sleep in their beds at the little cabin, so they loaded everyone on the tractor with a headlamp beaming to light the way back down to the Nenana River Valley.

    The following morning and for the next week and a half, the men had the same routine while the woman stayed at the cabin.

The Franklin Family Odyssey

By the second week all the logs were down on the ground, the footings were oiled and placed in the ground at the corners.

The days quickly shortened and the family knew they had plenty to do before the first snow fell which was predicted my October 15. Because of the imminent weather, the family returned to Fairbanks for food and supplies.

The next morning in Fairbanks the family went shopping. Later that morning the three male homesteaders and the twins traveled back to Ferry on the train leaving the three ladies in Fairbanks. The men arrived at the river with their supplies that evening, and a light snow had begun to fall.

The twins thought this development was really great so immediately they began sliding and playing in the fresh fallen snow near the railroad tracks. After a few minutes of frolicking, the adults got impatient with the boys, so John firmly suggested that they should come and help unload the supplies so

The Franklin Family Odyssey

the team could get inside to rest before a hard day to follow.

When John woke up the next morning, he looked out the window of the cabin and his jaw dropped. It had snowed over a foot and it was still snowing. He told Johnny, Jack and the twins to sleep in. After breakfast Jack went out to check the trail and he ran into Devere doing the same.

Devere called out, "So you guys stuck inside today?"

"Not sure, yet. How much snow you think?"

"I think you all need to rest a couple of days. I'll try to clear the hill up there so you boys can get back to your homestead."

Jack interrupted, "You don't have to do that, We can..."

Devere inserted, "My tractor, I'll do it. The big machine can handle the rest of the way if I get the hill cleared. Not a problem for

The Franklin Family Odyssey

me. Do it for the miners in the spring."

"It snows here in the spring?"

"You never know when....Supposed to quit soon...Hope we don't get a south wind after this."

"South wind?" Jack asked.

"You will find out about the south wind...... someday."

Jack shook his head and walked back to the cabin. He turned around abruptly when he heard the tractor start up. Devere revved the engine to a high rpm, then the tractor started to move slowly with a snow plow attachment on the front. He headed across the tracks and turned left up the steep hill slowly pushing snow. Soon the vehicle was out of sight. Jack could hear the dull sound of the vehicle as it moved up the incline.

Denny stuck his head out the door of the cabin and asked, "Mr. Jack, what was that sound we just heard?"

The Franklin Family Odyssey

Jack slipped past Denny into the house they he answered, "Devere is plowing the snow on the hill for us so we can get back to work in a couple of days. He figures we're stuck here at least a couple of days without working at the homestead."

John inserted, "Maybe that's good but maybe not."

Johnny spoke, "I wonder how Becka is doing. I guess the two moms can handle any problems. I miss my wife already."

Jack and John both laughed out-loud.

John told the twins to climb up into the loft and put their new winter gear on so they could enjoy the snowy weather outside. As quickly as their dad spoken they were up the ladder and back down with their gear on.

Johnny was assigned to go outside with his brothers to supervise for a while so he put on his gear as well. The snow was falling lighter than earlier, and the twins headed

The Franklin Family Odyssey

directly to the river a quarter of a mile away.

Their older brother ran swiftly after them and he yelled. "Stay close, Denny, Donald!!"

When the older brother caught up with his siblings, they were on the bank of the Nenana River attempting to walk on the newly formed ice.

"Denny and Donald don't walk on the ice. It's very thin."

The twins stopped abruptly and turned around to look at their older brother. Denny asked, "Thin ice?"

Out of breath Johnny answered, "Yes... thin ice. Let's go back closer to the cabin and have a snow ball fight."

Donald inserted, "That's no fun. The snow won't make snow balls. What's wrong with this stuff?"

Johnny answered, "It's too cold for

snow ball fighting. Let's just go back and find something to slide on the snow."

The three brothers returned to the road near Devere's. They looked around the yard for something they could drag each other with on the snowy road. They found an old sled with a rope attached to it. The twins took turns pulling each other while Johnny watched.

After a couple of hours of pulling the sled in the heavy dry snow, the twins thought it might be time for some hot soup for lunch. The three brothers covered with wet snow barged through the door into the little cabin looking for a meal. They demanded hot soup.

Jack and John had anticipated the soon return of the three wet brothers. The older Franklin told his brothers to dry out near the fire while Johnny served up the soup. Big John and Jack Jones were already at the table drinking some coffee in preparation for lunch.

When lunch was completed, John

The Franklin Family Odyssey

Franklin asked his boys to help him chop up some fire wood in the back of the cabin. Jack volunteered to help as well, while Johnny cleaned up the dishes.

After finishing the dishes, Johnny found his clan chopping firewood behind the cabin. He grabbed an ax to help split the wood.

Denny and Donald carried arm loads of split firewood into the cabin and place them in a pile near the stove. As they turned to get another load they heard a scream coming from the back of the cabin. They hurried out to check and see what was happening.

When the twins returned to where the adults were working, they saw their older brother on the ground holding his head. Big John had wrapped a heavy rag around his oldest son's wound to stop the bleeding from the back of his head.

Denny called out, "What happen, Dad? Is he alright?"

The Franklin Family Odyssey

At first John didn't answer because he and Jack were carrying Johnny toward the door of the cabin. He turned his head back to Denny and asked, "Can you boys open the door for us. We need to get this bleeding stopped."

Johnny was almost passed out when the two men laid his limp body on the floor of the little cabin. The family knew they needed to tend to this emergency right here and right now, since the largest town was over a hundred miles away from Ferry.

Quickly John tended to his oldest son. In the mean time Jack gathered the twins over next to the stove and the threesome began a prayer vigil for Johnny Franklin.

Within an hour John had Johnny resting comfortably in one of the beds in the cabin. The bleeding was under control and the oldest son was talking a bit.

"What happen," Johnny muttered.

The Franklin Family Odyssey

John answered softly, "My ax head flew off the handle and I guess in plunked you in the back of the head while you were picking up firewood. You received a nasty blow to the head."

Denny responded, "Do you need something for your headache? Can you drink anything, big brother?"

At first Johnny didn't respond. Then he mumbled, "I could use something hot. I'm shivering."

Denny and Donald quickly fixed him some hot tea and John propped Johnny up so he could drink. The patient seemed to react positively to the hot brew.

Two days later John and Jack decided it would be safe to drive the tractor all the way to the homestead. Johnny was still in bed with a really bad headache from his accident.

The twins were excited to get going since they were literally confined to a small cabin for two days. The two boys and two men fired the tractor up about eight AM and according to Devere's thermometer outside his doorway, it was 10 degrees below zero with a slight wind blowing.

By the time the team arrived at the homestead, they estimated that the temperature had risen at least 20 degrees and the wind was blowing very hard. The snow under their feet became very mushy and the borrowed vehicle got stuck several times pulling logs out of the woods.

Jack jumped off the tractor into a puddle of water and spoke, "I see what Devere was talking about. Instant spring in the middle of Alaska in the middle of winter."

John quickly responded, "Yea. I think maybe we'd better quit for the day. I wonder if this weather is going to continue?"

"According to our host down at the river, it should be snowing again tomorrow or the next." Jack answered.

The Franklin Family Odyssey

The foursome packed up their gear and jumped on the tractor and headed to their Ferry home.

Off and on for the next few weeks the team had to stay in the cabin for days at a time. Some slack time came from very cold weather. Other days they were delayed because of several feet of snow, but the cabin gradually was being formed. At one time there was three feet of snow on the cabin floor with walls up eight feet, but the roof was not completed.

Johnny slowly recovered from his head incident but wasn't able to help the crew much. Within a few weeks the men completed the roof and began working on the resident's inside so the ladies could return to the homestead from the city as soon as possible.

The Franklin Family Odyssey

The men returned to Fairbanks a few days before Thanksgiving and the families prepared for the baby to be born later in December. Little Johnny was born on December 21, Both families celebrated the birth of Jesus and the birth of a baby Franklin.

chapter five

the spring, short summer and next long winter

Every year in Alaska the Winters and the Summers are each a little different. Many times Springs are cool and cloudy. Once every ten years you may see a Summer with 90 degrees plus in the Nenana River Valley.

This particular Spring/ Summer was a long time coming and Jack and John were looking forward to a dry season so they could finish up the work around the first cabin, get a garden started early and build the Franklin's cabin. In the north, for a garden, early is June 1st or later.

This particular year, March was icy and wet. The gentlemen had their first run in with river overflow.

Overflow is the phenomenon of melting snow on a warm Spring day flowing over ice

The Franklin Family Odyssey

fields and then at night re-freezing in weird shapes and forms, and usually not on a level plane.

Jack and John soon discovered tractors don't quite transverse ice flows very well and most vehicles can't be navigated through and on overflow.

One early Spring day Johnny and Jack were transporting supplies across the frozen Nenana River at night. They drove out into the river and noticed a bit of moisture on the river near the shore. The two friends got off the vehicle and walked out onto the ice.

The further they walked, the deeper the water flowed on top of the ice. Jack decided very quickly that they should wait to finish this task another day and make sure the ice was still thick enough for the tractor's weight.

After discussing the situation with Devere the next day, the duo discovered that what they had encountered was just an overflow of fresh water from an open spot on

The Franklin Family Odyssey

the river upstream. The vehicle was able to cross the river that day but the following week the river was almost open right there at the bridge.

After this incident and a lot of thought and discussion (and in an attempt to be more independent from Devere's tractor), John purchased a world war two Jeep on one Spring trip to Fairbanks. He was excited when it was delivered by train to the Ferry side of the river a couple of weeks later.

In middle April the family prepared for the move to the first completed cabin. The newly obtained Jeep would come in handy in the next few weeks.

The cabin on the homestead was finally ready to be occupied by May first. John had promised Devere that the two families would be out of his little cabin, so he could rent the cabin to his yearly occupants that arrived in early May.

Though it was wet and sloppy on the

The Franklin Family Odyssey

trail in April, May was a bit drier. It took the family two weeks, using their newly acquired Jeep, to move completely and to settle down in the homestead cabin with six adults, two very large teenage boys and a baby

When all the moving had been completed, John and Jack decided they would take the family outside and pray a prayer of dedication for their new residence. Both families contributed testimonies of the success they had this last winter giving glory to the God who created the universe and they were all thankful for the home He had given them the strength to build.

Immediately after the little ceremony and prayer, John, Jack and Johnny began planning and preparing for winter. They decided that they needed to cut several cords of wood for their winter warmth, haul water and repair and purchase tools to make it through a short or a long winter.

Johnny was in charge of building a small wood shed with left over building logs and

The Franklin Family Odyssey

some tarp material they had purchased earlier in the month. He decided he would dig several holes and place an eight foot pole in the ground every several feet and they wrap the tarp around for walls to protect from blowing snow.

Later that week when the walls were ready, Johnny and his father put a roof on the shed with poles and left over brush that was piled fairly thick so that moisture would not seep into the freshly cut firewood.

The next day the woodshed was completed and the twins began stacking wood in the shelter. Off and on during this chore, rain showers fell on the work crew.

The three men and twin boys stayed very busy during June and July. The woodshed was packed to the top with firewood and immediately the two families started preparation for the second cabin on the forty acre plot just a mile from Jack's homestead cabin.

The Franklin Family Odyssey

John and Alice decided they wanted a larger cabin with at least one separate bedroom and a place where the whole family could eat at one time. They panned a five hundred square foot log cabin with a lean-to bedroom for themselves off the side of the cabin.

During the construction of the second cabin it was difficult to find adequate sized logs for the plan they had prepared. John had to use the jeep and pull logs, sometimes a few miles away to get the size they needed.

Another factor that slowed the team's progress was the fact that the wind blew heavily and it rained almost every day of August.

The large group of people were stuck inside most of the day, consequently it created stress for everyone involved. Johnny and Becka with the baby, went outside as much as possible while the twins were always ready to go anywhere, even in the rain, to play some kind of game.

The Franklin Family Odyssey

One evening when the young Franklin couple had arrived back to the cabin after a short wet reprise, they walked in on a loud discussion between Jack and big John. Becka's mom was crying and telling the group she wanted to go back to California before the winter began.

Becka and Johnny stood there for a few seconds in shock. Jack grabbed his wife's hand and quickly took her out into the rain. Later Johnny heard the jeep start up and he looked out of the window as his father-in-law drove the vehicle off the homestead.

Becka quickly found a place to sit near the fire to dry out. She covered her face and began to sob. Then she spoke through the tears, "The baby is so young and he won't know his grandparents. What...I"

Johnny quickly responded, "I don't know, sweetheart. We will talk to them when they return. I'm sure everything will be OK. Won't it be, Dad?"

The Franklin Family Odyssey

"Sure enough, Son. This little cabin is driving everyone a little crazy. Let's take some time to pray for Mary. Her mom is not doing very well according to the letter she just received."

Just as the group began to pray Denny and Donald pushed in through the front door. Big John asked them to join them as they held hands in a circle and prayed for their friends, Mary and her mother. When the prayer was completed they hugged each other and continued praying quietly for the difficult situation.

Two hours later, Johnny heard the noise of a vehicle arriving at the homestead. Quickly he ran outside into the twilight to check on Jack and Mary. The couple had smiles on their faces as they greeted the other family members.

Mary and Jack assured their daughter that they would be there for a few more weeks to love and spoil the little baby. Becka's father also announced that they had to go back to California to take care of Mary's mom who was very ill. The couple didn't rule out coming back to Alaska later, but they told Johnny that they were going to arrange to sign their property and the cabin over to him and Becka.

Jack spoke softly, "Johnny, my incredible son in law, you are the man to take care of the forty acres and grow a great family there. I'm excited for you, and remember if we do return, even for a visit, keep a place for Mary and I."

Johnny grabbed his father in law and hugged him. Becka came near and shared in the group love.

Later in the week the men of the two families returned to work on the second cabin in between rain storms.

In early September the first snow began to fall and it didn't quit for two solid weeks. Two feet of snow had piled up on the beginnings of the new lodging for the John

The Franklin Family Odyssey

Franklin's family.

Jack and Alice Jones temporarily moved out of the crowded cabin and into Fairbanks to began preparations for their return to the lower forty eight in late October.

Finally, by the first of October the Jones' cabin was almost completed accept for the interior. Their goal was for this second cabin to be ready to be occupied by December. Everything was on schedule until out of nowhere a heavy south wind began blowing in the Ferry area. The temperature increased to almost fifty degrees and naturally the snow that had already fallen was melting rapidly.

The trails were flooded with water and lots of over flow blocked the access to the homestead area. Consequently, the Franklin families decided to join the Jones for two weeks in Fairbanks before Becka's parent's trip south.

At the bed and breakfast in Fairbanks,

The Franklin Family Odyssey

Jack and Mary finalized their plans to head south with the truck that they had driven north over a year earlier. Mary was told that her mother didn't have long to live so they had to hurry if they planned on seeing her before she passed.

The day of the Jones' trip, John and the rest of the family prayed for the traveler's protection. At the time of departure, Mary and Jack held their grandson one last time, hugged their daughter and son-in-law, and gave John and Alice a loving goodbye. They then climbed into the packed truck and started their journey south. Jack was fully prepared for a long, late fall trip on the Alaskan Highway.

Becka cried as they left and spoke through her sobs, "Please, Jesus, protect my mom and dad. Bring them back to see little Johnny. Please, Lord."

Johnny quickly inserted, "They'll be back. Your mom loves it here. It's just hard on her having her mother sick a couple thousand miles away. I predict we will have a welcoming back party in a very short time."

John responded, "I agree, son, but let's keep praying about that and for their protection in the mean time. You know, I believe God can heal Mary's mom. Yes I do."

Chapter six
moving in and the baby

Becka sat in her newly built rocking chair and held her new born little boy. The young mother's face was damp with tears due to her constant physical pain. In addition, she grieved with an inner pain because she missed her mom and dad terribly.

The hurting wife watched through her tears as the twins and Johnny worked intently on the cabin kitchen, building cabinets and counters out of freshly cut spruce.

From time to time Johnny checked on Becka's physical pain and he kept insisting that she lie down rather than sit in her upright chair. The young mother continued to say she was OK, and wanted to watch him work, but her husband knew better.

Becka observed intently as Johnny created, according to her specifications, a huge pantry for their back up food supply and she smiled broadly when the twins and her husband carried her brand new wood cook stove into the area right under the stove pipe that went through the ceiling.

When the long work day was completed, Johnny took his turn holding the baby and tending to him while Becka stretched out in the bed to rest her weary body that seemed to be giving up on her.

Johnny put Junior into his newly built crib and covered him gently. He then turned to his ailing wife whose head was covered with her pillow.

The worried husband asked, "Becka, is there anything I can do? My heart aches for you because I really don't know what to do for

The Franklin Family Odyssey

your pain."

Becka mumbled, "I don't know...You can pray for me. Johnny, I miss my mom and dad. I hope they are safe. Pray for me and for them, please."

"OK, Jesus, we love you. Becka and I are so thankful you have been so good to us but, right now Becka is in pain in more ways than one. I believe you can heal my beautiful wife and comfort her. We don't even know what's wrong with her but you do. Heal her body and restore her. Also, Lord, keep the family safe in every circumstance they might be in. Bring them back to us, soon. Thank you, Lord."

Becka rolled over on her back and smiled at her husband then she spoke, "Thank you, dear husband. I feel better already, but can I stay in bed for a while?"

"I'll fix you some soup and bread. How's that? Before you sleep."

"You can warm me up some soup. That

The Franklin Family Odyssey

would be nice. Johnny, do you really believe my mom and dad will be coming back to Alaska? That's what you prayed."

"Becka, I believe they will be back soon. We haven't heard from them, but that doesn't mean anything. Mark my word, they will be back by next winter and maybe before. I know that's a brave statement but....I believe it."

"You sure know how to make a girl feel so much better. Thank you, dear husband."

The next morning Johnny was the first one up to tend to Johnny Junior. He carried the baby around and rocked him in the rocking chair until Becka stirred around and offered to feed the baby.

Johnny was fixing breakfast for himself and his wife when he heard a soft knock on the front door of the cabin. The young father called as he flipped the hot cakes on the griddle, "Come in...Is that you Denny and Donald? Have you guys eaten breakfast yet?"

The Franklin Family Odyssey

The front door opened slowly. Alice Franklin meekly looked around the door and waved to her son."

"Mom, what are you doing here? I mean we love it when you visit us but it is really early."

Johnny dropped his spatula on the table, wiped his hands with a towel, and quickly hugged his mom. He spoke again, "Mom, is there something wrong? Dad, the twins....are they OK?"

Alice spoke softly, "I...I just came to check on Becka. The twins hinted that she still wasn't feeling well. Is she sleeping?"

"No, she's feeding the baby right now. Yes, she is feeling rather poorly. I prayed for her last night and she seemed to be doing better after that. This morning....? I'm not too sure. Been working on breakfast. You want some?"

"I taught you well....no, I've already

The Franklin Family Odyssey

eaten and the twins should be coming over soon. Can I go check on your sweet wife?"

"Go right in. She will be glad to see you."

Alice Franklin softly knocked on the bedroom door and opened it slowly. Then she spoke. "Becka, it's Alice. Can I come in for a minute?"

Becka answered, "Oh, what a surprise. Come on in. I was just feeding little Johnny. Is everything OK with you?"

"I heard from the twins that you weren't doing very well. I thought maybe I could help a little around here while you were bedridden. What's a mother-in-law here for?"

"That's really sweet of you. Did you ask Johnny? He's been doing a lot around here, lately. He prayed for me yesterday. I feel much better today. I've been really missing my parents. Johnny strongly feels they will come back to Alaska by winter. I pray he's right but if they don't it's alright. God is in control."

"You have a great spirit, Becka. God is in control. Being in the wilderness like this is kind of hard for us women, but God can bring us through. He's helped me so much. I think your mom had a hard time here in Alaska, but I heard my husband say that he believed they would come back soon, as well."

"Wow, I just got a chill up my spine. I feel you just spoke a word from the Lord. Alice, I mean Mom, you are a blessing."

Alice hugged her daughter-in-law for a few minutes and began to say her goodbyes when Denny and Donald barged into the small cabin bedroom.

Denny blurted out, "Mom, we were wondering where you were. We had to fix our own breakfast and Donald is very sorry he left a mess on the stove."

Donald, behind Denny, grabbed his brother by his shirt collar and pulled him back

The Franklin Family Odyssey

into the living area. Then he spoke, "Wait a minute, brother. Who made the mess? Mom!! We both made a mess but we did clean it up, sort of."

Alice looked at her two sons in disgust, then started laughing. Becka joined her in her amusement.

Johnny piped in, "You guys are something else. It's been this way for years. Mom, was I this bad?"

Mrs. Franklin did not respond to her oldest son's question. Instead she said, "I guess I'd better get back to the cabin and clean up a mess in my kitchen. I'll keep praying for Becka, son. You take good care of her. You, twins, behave and help your big brother get this place completed." She called back to Becka, "Bye, my daughter, young Becka."

Baby Johnny grew quickly while his mom became physically stronger and healthier. It was already March and outside it was still cold. Becka hadn't left the cabin in weeks.

The Franklin Family Odyssey

"Johnny, what will we do for Easter this year? I need to get out of this cabin. Sweetheart, can we go to Fairbanks for church on Easter? Would that be too difficult?"

"Believe it or not, my parents and I were going to ask you if you were up to traveling sometime soon....Like Easter. We are almost done with the building here around the cabin and we need to get some supplies to make it through the summer and to get the garden going. Sounds like a mouth full, but yes we can."

Becka laid little Johnny down and ran with her arms wide open toward her husband. She hugged and kissed him while Johnny swung her in a circle and set her in a chair at the kitchen table then he spoke, "It sure is great having you healthy. It will be an even greater Easter season and a wonderful Spring."

"Maybe by then Mom and Dad will be coming back to Alaska. That's what I've been praying."

The Franklin Family Odyssey

"My Dad heard a rumor, or maybe a hint about that in a letter from your Dad. The estate is closing and they will have plenty of income to come back. We will see, soon. It will be up to your mom. You've heard from her, haven't you?"

"Yea, but she still wasn't sure...but I am. Johnny, I love you."

Johnny Franklin smiled at his wife then someone knocked at their front door. Becka walked slowly to the door and opened it.

"Johnny, it's your Mom and Dad and the twins...Come in, family. What a surprise. Husband, did you know they were coming?"

Johnny answered immediately, "Maybe."

Alice inserted, "We kind of invited ourselves. We brought dinner with us. Home fried chicken and the fixings. We thought you would appreciate a little family time without all the work. Bring in the food, Denny and Donald."

The Franklin Family Odyssey

John, Denny and Donald had their hands full of chicken, mashed potatoes, gravy and vegetables. Johnny smiled broadly while he helped set the table and find everyone a chair to get the big dinner started.

The Franklin family feasted and visited for almost an hour when John Franklin held his arms up and brought silence into the room. He had something important to say.

"I have somewhat of an announcement to make. Some of you might already know this but others don't...First of all Easter is just a little over a month from now. Two things are happening. We all are going into Fairbanks and we will go to our favorite church for Easter Sunday. We have many friends there, that we haven't seen in months. Becka hasn't been out of the house in months. She's probably anxious to get out and about."

Becka announced, "I'm ready."

Alice added, "I think we are all ready."

The Franklin Family Odyssey

Johnny looked at his father and said, "Continue, Dad."

John Franklin spoke, "Becka, this will be a surprise to you. That weekend your mom and dad will be waiting for us at church. They will arrive from the lower forty-eight that week. I just learned that Mary got a substantial inheritance and they are arranging to have a cabin built in the area and possibly one in Fairbanks as well."

"Wow!!" Becka echoed, with her hands raised in the air. "Mom and Dad are coming back. My husband was prophetic and God you are so good."

Johnny stood up slowly and began to speak, "I think it would be appropriate for all of us to join hands and pray for the Jones as they travel. Can we?"

The family members each pushed their chairs back and stood. Baby Johnny whined in the bedroom so Becka quickly left and returned with the little one. They all joined

The Franklin Family Odyssey

hands and John Franklin prayed a powerful prayer followed by Johnny's closing thankfulness to God.

Alice, John and the twins prepared to head back to their cabin. Becka and Johnny hugged them all, then Becka grabbed Johnny and whispered in his ear.

The young mother announce, "Family, Easter Sunday Johnny and I want to dedicate baby Johnny to the Lord in our church there. Does that sound great?"

Everyone in unison were pleased with the announcement.

"Then that's a plan," the young mother inserted. "That means we need to get to Fairbanks a day early so I can find a new outfit for my big boy and his daddy."

Johnny spoke, "Sounds good to me."

The whole family laughed, cheered and hugged as the Franklin's departed.

The Franklin Family Odyssey

The month of march went by quickly for the whole Franklin family as they prepared to journey to Fairbanks a few days before Easter.

The weather in the north land was in the 40's and it was a very sloppy day when the family traveled down the hill to catch the train at Ferry.

In a few hours they were all settled into the bed and breakfast they always stayed in when visiting Fairbanks. The Jones hadn't arrive yet but they were expected within a day or two.

The whole family went shopping in a light mist that covered the Chena Valley. Johnny Junior got a cute little suit and a bow tie.

It took Johnny Senior a little longer to find something appropriate for Easter but Becka finally convinced him to buy a tie and some nice slacks. The young father wasn't used to wearing a tie or slacks at all.

The Franklin Family Odyssey

John and Alice did their best to outfit the twins for church but Donald and Denny fought their parents all day long. The twins decided on new jeans and a white shirts. They even had matched outfits for the big Easter event.

The Franklin Family Odyssey

Chapter seven

the reunion

Becka was very excited to see her parents as they parked their new truck on the street near the bed and breakfast where the family was staying for the Easter weekend. Her physical malady was long gone and Becka was again a beautiful, enthusiastic young mother.

Jack and Mary arrived in Fairbanks Saturday morning to a light rain. They pulled into the city a little later than they had planned. The Alaska Highway had given Jack and his wife their share of grief for the last two weeks. The Jones were happy to not be traveling on the day before Easter.

The Jones and the Franklins took up a whole pew in the third row at the beautiful First Evangelical Church that Easter

The Franklin Family Odyssey

Sunday morning. The family shared hymn books as they sang with enthusiasm and fervor. They particularly liked "He Arose," the song many churches sing on Easter.

After service in the church lobby, the families greeted many old friends and then quickly ran to their vehicles in the pouring down rain. The twins led the way, running and skipping. Then they stopped abruptly at the Franklin's vehicle.

Johnny Franklin, carrying an umbrella for Becka and the baby, did not see his twin brother's abrupt stop. He ran right into Donald and fell to the street with the umbrella in his hand. Becka immediately handed her baby to her mom and went directly to Johnny lying in the road.

John Franklin could see from his viewpoint that Johnny's right leg was broken so he and Jack carefully lifted Johnny up put the young Franklin into the back of the Jones' new truck. Donald held

The Franklin Family Odyssey

the umbrella over his brother in the back of the truck. The rest of the family loaded into the Franklins' truck and they drove quickly to the local hospital.

After an emergency surgery and several hours wait, the doctors let Becka know that Johnny would be in the hospital for a few days and that he would be in a full leg cast for a few months.

The Franklins easily concluded that they would stay at least a month in Fairbanks at the bed and breakfast. This worked well for the Jones because they wanted to find some land near the city and possibly start building a house before winter arrived.

Johnny had a rough two weeks with severe pain and an uncomfortable stay in Fairbanks General. The third week he was finally able to go back to the bed and breakfast. Johnny rested better with his family, than he did at the hospital.

The Franklin Family Odyssey

The young Franklin had to return to the medical facility several times in the next few weeks for physical therapy on his broken leg. He was ready to head back to the homestead but his doctor decided Johnny needed at least three to five weeks in Fairbanks.

In the mean time, Jack and Mary found a good piece of property for a reasonable price north of the city in the woods. Mr. Jones solicited John Franklin and his twins to help him begin the task of constructing a good size cabin on the ten acres that they purchased.

The four men came home to the bed and breakfast every evening, warn to a frazzle, but the team accomplished a great deal as Johnny recuperated from is messed up leg.

The ladies, Mary, Alice and Becka, had lots of time to travel around Fairbanks viewing the historical sites as well as checking out all the dress shops in the

The Franklin Family Odyssey

Chena Valley.

As Spring moved into June, John told Jack that he and the twins needed to get back out to Ferry to start gathering wood and begin preparing for winter. Johnny was disappointed that he wasn't ready to help his family. The ladies were happy to remain at the bed and breakfast.

Every other week Johnny had doctor appointments and the twins and John came back from Ferry to help the ladies get the injured man back and forth to the hospital. Even with a crude wheel chair it wasn't easy for all those involved, especially Johnny.

On his last scheduled visit before their prospective return to Ferry in late June, the doctor informed the family that Johnny needed at least another three weeks because apparently he re-broke one of the bones that was previously fractured.

Johnny and John were very

The Franklin Family Odyssey

disappointed about this setback because Fall was approaching and the family had planned an extensive moose hunt which included Jack Jones. John suggested to everyone that God had a perfect plan and that all things work together for good to then that love God and are called according to His purpose.

Johnny timidly smiled and spoke, "Dad, I remember you and Mom quoting that verse so many times when I was a kid. I not only hear what you are saying, I agree. That was from God. I needed it."

Becka, carrying baby Johnny, walked up to Johnny who sat in his wheel chair. She snuggled up close to her husband and then responded, "Can I be prophetic. I say you will be either with the guys or right close by when they bag the first moose. God is the healer and I believe it."

Everyone said a hearty Amen and they all gathered around Johnny to pray. Jack led the prayer.

The Franklin Family Odyssey

"Dear, God, we all gathered here together in your name. We believe you are the great healer. Work miracles today with my dear son-in-law so he can participate somehow and someway with our coming moose hunt. Thank you, Lord. Amen."

It was late July and the three weeks went by quickly for the family; everyone but Johnny.

The moose hunt which would start September 1, was just a little over a month away. Becka kept noticing that baby Johnny wasn't sleeping very well at night. In fact, he was coughing and had a lot of congestion. She took him to her lady doctor that had an office around the corner from the bed and breakfast.

Dr. Jane was very concerned and gave the baby some antibiotics. She asked Becka to bring him back in a few days.

When the young mother arrived

The Franklin Family Odyssey

home from the appointment, she gathered the family together again to pray for baby Johnny.

The Franklin men, except Johnny were still working at Ferry. Their goal was to complete the winter preparation by September first, but they really wanted to finish a few days before moose season started.

Two days later the men arrived back to the bed and breakfast for Johnny's next appointment. Becka asked John to pray for her baby and when the prayer was finished, she felt it reached heaven.

Mary walked with her daughter over to the doctor's office the very next day. The ladies were anticipating a good report from the doctor. Dr. Jane thoroughly checked the baby and told his mother that baby Johnny seemed to react really well to the antibiotics.

The female doctor suggested that

The Franklin Family Odyssey

when they returned to Ferry, to monitor little Johnny closely for congestion. She thought he might have asthma or something like it. She told Becka that the baby seemed to be much better than a few days earlier. The young mother knew their prayers brought the swifter recovery for her baby.

That evening after the family had a time of rejoicing for baby Johnny's good doctor's report, big Johnny was really tired and went to bed earlier than the rest of the family. A few hours later after wishing the rest of the family a goodnight, Becka returned to her bedroom where Johnny and baby Johnny were fast asleep.

Becka notice that baby Johnny's breathing was almost normal and she whispered a thank you prayer for his healing as she crawled into bed. Snuggling close to her semi-crippled husband, the young wife noticed Johnny was really restless.

The Franklin Family Odyssey

The next morning about four AM, baby Johnny woke up as usual and his mom quickly went to her son before the noise disturbed big Johnny's sleep.

Becka began feeding the baby and big Johnny called out to Becka, "Hey, sweetheart, how's the baby? He sounds good. His breathing that is."

Becka answered, "Sorry we woke you, Johnny. He's doing great. God is good."

"Becka, I need to talk to you for a minute. Can you do that and talk as well?"

"I'm almost done, dear. I'll be right with you."

The baby was done eating and had gone back to sleep so Becka put him back in his bassinet and returned to bed next to Johnny.

Becka asked, "What did you want to talk about, Johnny. Are you OK? so you need pain medicine?"

Johnny shook the cobwebs from his head and began, "Yea, I...I don't know if I told you about my dreams."

Becka interrupted, "You have dreams? I dream everyday but don't remember most of them."

"This dream is different. When I was young I had this dream all the time. I spoke to my dad about it years ago because at that time I didn't understand. Well, I didn't know where Alaska was for one thing."

"So your dream is about Alaska? What about Alaska?"

"I'm trying to tell you, sweetheart. This is complicated. I believe some dreams are symbolic and they come from God like the dreams in the Bible that Daniel and Joseph had. The pharaoh in Egypt had symbolic dreams as well as others. But other dreams are literal and could be...and I emphasis could be actual occurrences that happen in the future."

Again Becka interrupted, "Are you telling me, you had a dream about us, way back when you were a kid."

"Basically I guess you are right. I dreamed I was married with a baby and we lived in a place a long way from nowhere in a land in the far north. I'm afraid to tell you the rest of the dream."

The young wife frowned and then asked, "Why are you afraid to tell me. Now you're scaring me."

"Well, it's kind of scary but has a happy ending. Should I continue or do you want to hear this later?"

"I'm not so sure either way, but you might as well finish or it will drive me crazy thinking about it," Becka commented.

"OK, I will finish," Johnny sighed deeply and again spoke, "This is going to

The Franklin Family Odyssey

be hard to do but here goes. We are married and were living in our log cabin in the woods of Alaska. We loved our life with our baby but one warm summer things got really bad. It was a very dry year and the forest around us was ready to catch on fire with just a small spark from anything. Every evening during this summer lightning storms with very little rain surrounded the valley in which we lived."

Becka covered her face and then spoke, "Don't tell me? A fire surrounded our cabin and we had to leave it and it burned down?"

"Not quite like that. I told you this would be hard. You and I are outside clearing brush around the cabin. The fire wasn't that far away so we were making a fire break. The whole sky was full of smoke and I prepared barrels of water nearby in case of fire."

Johnny stopped to take another deep

breath and then he continued, "That evening the fires were burning very close and the roof of the cabin caught on fire as I carried the baby out of the house. You were right behind me. We got away from it. I tried to put the fire out but the whole place burnt down."

"Johnny!! What!! Were we OK, afterwards? In your dream, that is."

"Let me finish, Becka. I get you both out and Johnny was a little sick from the smoke. That's all I can remember. I think that is where the dream ended."

"You are scaring me, Johnny. Would God allow this to happen? I don't want to go back to the cabin if this happens."

Johnny pulled his wife as close as he could and continued, "God is in control. We will build another cabin if this happens. I know this is scary. Can you imagine, I've been holding this inside for a few years praying that it wasn't real. I'm still not sure it is..accept everything else has happened so far."

Becka, still in Johnny's arms began to weep then Johnny prayed, "God, please help my dear wife and give her the peace she needs to live through uncertainty. You are in control and I believe, as my dad taught me. All things work together for good to them that love God and are called according to His purpose. Amen."

The Franklin Family Odyssey

Chapter eight

The deadly hunt and the early but easy winter

John Franklin and his family, including Johnny, Becka and little Johnny, returned to their cabins just north of Ferry. It wasn't easy getting a tall man with a large cast on his leg, up through the woods three miles to his cabin in the wilderness.

For the Franklin family it had been a long time since they had been back to their real home, but they were glad to be there. Earlier that summer John, Donald and Denny cut and gathered wood for both cabins so they could make it through the upcoming winter. At that time they also prepared for their annual moose hunting adventure which would begin shortly.

Big Johnny got healthier and stronger by the day, as hunting season approached. The twins helped their big brother get

The Franklin Family Odyssey

around and exercise. Becka kept reminding Johnny of the prophetic word she had given him right after he broke his leg.

Meanwhile just north of Fairbanks, Jack and Mary, with help from hired carpenters and log home builders, were rapidly completing their large cabin.

Unfortunately, as the Jones were finishing up the roof of their project, thunderstorms encompassed the whole area with many lightning strikes and a half an inch of rain. According to reports the lightning started a few fires on the edge of Fairbanks.

Mr. Jones was anxious about the fires nearby their construction site so he temporarily shut down his job and decided to take Mary back to Ferry. Before he left Fairbanks, Jack checked into fire insurance for his property which was just introduced nationwide.

The Jones arrived in Ferry the day before moose season opened. After arriving, Jack got his new gun ready with a little target practice. He set his site and calibrated the new scope.

Mary went directly to Becka and Johnny's cabin to see the grandson while the men, including Johnny, packed their gear for hunting the next morning.

John had prepared his four wheel drive jeep with a large rack for the gear and decided to haul a trailer to bring the meat back. The team was planning to get an early start, so they all went to bed early.

The next morning, September 1st, long before sunup, Denny and Donald were dressed and had hurried out to the vehicle with their guns and ammunition. The first thing the twins noticed when they went outside was that it was very cold and cloudy and the weather was extremely threatening. The twins immediately decided they needed their winters coats instead of summer jackets.

John and Johnny, still inside, drank warm cups of coffee and ate a hearty breakfast. In the middle of bacon and eggs, Jack knocked on the door of John's cabin.

Jack was invited inside, and he immediately asked, "Got some of that hot stuff for me, too? It's really cold out here. It looks and feels like snow."

Johnny answered, "Come on in. I'll pour you some, Jack. Wants some breakfast?"

"I had a little cereal at Becka's house. I think I'm alright."

Jack sat next to John and across from Johnny. He wrapped his cold hands around the warm mug and sipped his hot beverage. Denny and Donald, with their winter gear on this time, were ready to go back out and start the hunting.

Denny asked, "You men ready to go shoot a big bull moose here soon? Donald and I are ready to fly."

John looked up from his breakfast and frowned at Denny, then he spoke, "I don't know about you, but I'm eating. I'll be ready when I'm ready. Remember I'm the driver."

The men all laughed as the twins plopped down on the living room couch to wait. With frowns on their faces, they weren't waiting very patiently.

A half an hour later the hunters were packed into the jeep; including Johnny with his small cast. The gear was backed on the roof of the vehicle and in the trailer.

The adults of the hunting team had already decided they would travel cross country toward Windy Creek, a tiny creek that came out of the hills and flowed into the Nenana River about a thousand feet below. Earlier in the year, the twins, on one of their adventures, spotted at least one bull moose and several cows in the area.

John drove carefully up the creek a couple of miles and found some larger trees where they could set up a base camp and then make themselves a tree stand.

The Franklin Family Odyssey

Johnny seemed to be doing OK with his healing leg but there wasn't much of a trail so the journey was very rough.

The team set up a base camp where Johnny could relax his leg and the young father could be ready with his own rifle. They also provided him a chair, some books, and a Bible.

The twins were anxious to get going on their own and to look for signs of the big one. John wasn't so sure that they were ready to be hiking this deep in the woods by themselves. Jack suggested that he would keep an eye on at least one of them for John.

The elder Franklin decided to team up with Denny and they hiked toward the north across the creek and up a steep ridge. Jack asked Donald to be his right hand man and they trekked west up the creek into the heavy forest.

Johnny readied his gun at the base camp and kept an eagle eye opened for game of any kind that would wander

The Franklin Family Odyssey

nearby. He wasn't sure how he would dress the game but he knew he could figure something out if it came down to that.

The first two days of the hunt, the two hunting teams hiked for miles over the hills and valleys near Windy Creek without spotting signs of any moose let alone a visual of a big bull.

In the evenings of the moose hunt, John and Jack related to the Franklin sons several hunting stories that they had participated in over the years. The boys asked many questions but Denny asked the most thought provoking one.

"Jack and Dad, have you ever been on a hunting trip where someone was shot accidentally? Sounds like a scary thing that could happen."

Jack quickly answered, "I...well, I guess it was, we; this other guy and I. We aren't sure who. Could have been me. Well, anyway a guy we didn't know, got shot out in the woods of Northern

The Franklin Family Odyssey

California. It was so bad. We didn't know what to do but God worked it all out. I don't like to talk about it."

John inserted, "Yea, Jack, I heard about that when we started building our cabin before Johnny was born. That must have been tough on you for the next year's hunt."

"Yea, it was, but God....He did it for me. Gave me peace."

Donald bowed his head and spoke, "I don't want that to happen to me. Jack, you will help me be careful?"

"That's my job. Let's get some sleep for an early hunt tomorrow. John, why don't you pray for our success for tomorrow."

John grabbed Denny and Donald's hands and prayed for the success and protection for the team the next day. When he said amen they noticed a few snowflakes falling from the night sky.

Jack called out, "Sleep warm tonight,

The Franklin Family Odyssey

guys. It could be white by morning."

The next morning the ground was white with a half an inch of snow that had fallen during the night. The hunters dressed warmly, drank a warm drink, ate a fast breakfast, and then began their exploring.

Johnny found a dry and warm place to keep watch at camp.

About an hour later, after they had began a steep climb up to the ridge, John and Denny began tracking what looked like a large bull moose that was walking along the ridge above the creek. The duo watched with their binoculars as it started to disappeared over the a nearby hill. Just as John raised his rifle to shoot, the team heard two gunshots that came from just south of their location.

The two Franklins heard what seemed like a commotion just below their position on the mountain. They hurried down the ridge to see if the movement was the other hunting party with some game.

The Franklin Family Odyssey

When Denny and his dad arrived at the bottom of the valley, they could see Donald crouching in the middle of the frozen creek, his gun in hand. Jack was a hundred feet up the creek standing next to a large bull moose lying on the edge of the woods.

John asked Donald, "Did you get a big buck? Is that yours up there where Jack is?"

Donald began to cry, turned around, dropped his gun on the ice and ran off.

The older Franklin called out to Jack, "What's up with Donald. Did he just shoot a bull up there?"

Jack walked slowly down to where Denny and John stood and then began, "We have a problem. I think we... shot another hunter...I mean Donald shot a hunter. Not that sure what happen. We saw him go down but we can't find him. I'm not sure if he's still alive or not. We got the bull but."

The Franklin Family Odyssey

"Well, Jack, we have a dilemma. It's cool enough but we probably should gut the game as soon as possible. Why don't you search for the hunter. Denny and I should find Donald before he hurts himself, then we will gut the moose."

Jack shook his head and quickly ran back up the creek to track the bloody path of the missing hunter.

The father and son crossed the creek and began looking for the distressed Donald. They found him a hundred yards into the forest and lovingly walked him back to the base camp to tell Johnny what had happened.

Johnny had Donald sit with him and the older brother began to pray for the twin. Johnny's dad and Denny quickly hurried back to the creek to dress and transport the moose back to base camp.

It was almost dark when John and Denny carried the last of the meat back to camp. John asked his sons if Jack had returned during the day. They told their

The Franklin Family Odyssey

dad they hadn't seen him at all. John Franklin was really worried.

Just as John had decided to head back out to look for Jack, their friend walked slowly into camp with his head down.

Jack announced to his friends, "I didn't find him or the body. I don't understand because I know we saw the guy fall after the shot. Didn't we, Donald?"

Donald lowered his head and spoke, "I think so. I've been really praying about this. I hope that guy is OK."

John thought for a second and then said, "God is in control. You did your best, Jack. And we've been out here three days. Those other hunters should have known we were here, I'm sure. There is no excuse for shooting someone but you looked for this guy and what else can we do."

Johnny answered, "Pray. That's it."

Consequently the five hunters decided they would leave for home early

The Franklin Family Odyssey

the next morning so Johnny volunteered to fend off the animals and protect their game during the night. Unfortunately the young father fell asleep on his watch.

During his lapse into sleep, Johnny's dream that he had visioned since he was young, returned in full color and in great detail. Suddenly Johnny woke up in a fright just like he had done many times in his short lifespan.

The young man was embarrassed that he had fallen asleep on his watch. He carefully got up and limped over to check on the meat that was hung from a tree nearby. Johnny didn't see the sign of any animal that had bothered their game but he still felt guilty that he fell asleep.

Just as Johnny slowly moved back to his spot in front of the dying fire, Donald crawled out of the tent and ran into the woods.

In shock Johnny followed his brother with his eyes. Within minutes the Franklin twin walked slowly back to the camp and

The Franklin Family Odyssey

wandered over to the fire. He grabbed a log that was lying nearby and put it on the fire.

Johnny asked his brother, "You OK, little brother? What was that all about?"

Donald sat down next to his brother. He took a stick and poked at the fire, then he responded, "Was a little sick and didn't want to through up in the tent or on Denny's head. Besides I needed to...You know what."

Johnny laughed and said, "Yea, I know. It's been a funny night for me too. I dozed off on my watch and had my famous dream again but this time in real color. I just keep praying, this is just a dream and not going to really happen. It has a happy ending but...."

"I had a dream, too." Donald inserted. "It was a rehearsal of what might happen if I really killed someone while hunting. I don't think I can go hunting again. I feel so..."

Johnny quickly interrupted, "Donald, I know this whole thing is tough on you but like we all have been saying the last few weeks and I know it's a cliche, but it's true, God is in control. You will survive this just like I am surviving my broken leg that happen because my twin brothers stopped so quickly in front of me in a pouring down rain."

Donald laughed and said, "We are truly sorry for that. Denny and I are always in a hurry. Yes, I will survive. Big brother, you are a good pray-er. Can you pray for me?"

The twin walked over to where his brother sat and knelt down. Johnny reached out, touched Donald, and prayed, "Dear, Jesus, You are in control. Donald and I know this. Work in my little brother and comfort him after this traumatic experience. Calm his heart and mind and assure him that you have everything in control. Thank You, Lord."

The Franklin Family Odyssey

Chapter nine

the nasty breakup

Becka opened the cabin door and looked out. The skies were black and the rain was torrential. The young mother quickly slammed the door tightly and went into her bedroom to check on a whining son.

The Franklin mother wondered, as she picked up little Johnny, where her husband was. It was close to the time that she and her husband had devotions together everyday. The young wife knew he was helping his dad with a leak in the pantry at his parents cabin, but that was hours ago.

A few minutes later while Becka fed the baby in the bedroom, Johnny walked in the door soak to the skin. He carefully took off his raincoat and hung it near the wood stove. He kicked off his wet boots

The Franklin Family Odyssey

and tip toed into the bedroom.

Johnny's wife rocked the baby while in a daze when the young Franklin appeared in the doorway.

Becka quipped, "Oh, you scared me, Johnny. I've been waiting for you. Was the leak really bad?"

Johnny quickly hugged her and the baby and then he answered, "Yea, food got wet. Ruined some of it. We still aren't done but at least the water isn't pouring into the house."

"Wow, that's good. I hope we don't..."

"I know, Becka, but your dad did a good job on this roof. I doubt if we....Wait a minute I here a..."

Together they screamed, "A drip.."

Johnny hurriedly ran into the kitchen. He watched as water dripped down the stove pipe on the kitchen wood stove. It turned quickly into steam on the stove top.

The Franklin Family Odyssey

From the bedroom Becka asked, "A leak, Johnny?"

"Down the stove pipe. I'll need to get up there at put some tar on the roof where the pipe comes through."

"Do you have to do it now? It's our devotion time. And I haven't seen you all day. It's so boring sitting in this cabin by myself with all this rain. It's supposed to be Spring....The baby wants to see his daddy...Huh, little Johnny?"

Johnny got a step stool and checked on the leak from the inside at the ceiling. He figured it wasn't too bad at that moment, but he wanted to keep an eye on it.

"I'll be right there. Get your Bible ready...Second Kings, remember?"

"I've already got it opened for us. Come on and hold Johnny while I read to you."

Johnny finished his task, put the step stool away, and returned to the bedroom.

The Franklin Family Odyssey

The baby reached out his arms for his daddy. Johnny grabbed his son and spun him around in a circle then quickly set down on the bed near Becka who was still rocking in the chair with the Bible in her lap.

Quickly they finished their devotions, prayed and Johnny put little Johnny in his homemade playpen. The young husband grabbed his wife's hand and walked her into the kitchen.

While holding Becka close, he showed her where the leak was and together they walked around to see if there was any other moisture breaches.

Johnny began, "So far so good, but after dinner I may have to go back to my parents place. I guess the twins are finished with their schooling and both of them are planning to go somewhere this evening. My parents may need my help."

"I'll be OK. You do what you have to. Your dad has helped us plenty of times."

The Franklin Family Odyssey

"I need to check on your parent's new cabin, just in case. It's really raining out there. Flooding everywhere. I also need to check the trail because we need to get supplies soon. Mom and Dad may have to restock what they lost."

Becka smiled and sent her husband a sly look, then she asked, "We're going to town? Sounds good to me. Do we have any money?"

Johnny stared at his wife and responded, "We have some money but you know neither of us are working and we live in the sticks on a homestead...What are you getting at?"

"Just wondering. We'll talk about it later when we are ready to go to town. Love you, Johnny."

"Love you, too, Becka."

Johnny hugged his wife again and checked on the baby. He went to the door and put his rain gear back on and addressed his wife, "I'll be back for dinner.

The Franklin Family Odyssey

My Dad and I can probably get this done swiftly. I'm hoping I won't have to go back later. Be back as soon as I can."

Becka blew him a kiss from the kitchen wood stove and replied, "Going to have a great dinner, hubby. You'll love it. See you in a bit."

Johnny smiled and exited into the wind and rain.

An hour and a half later, the younger Franklin returned to his little cabin finding his wife cooking a huge pot of moose stew with carrots and potatoes that they had canned the last summer.

"Sure smells good in here. Nice to be out of the wet. How's things?"

Becka put her spoon down after stirring the stew and replied, "I'm doing great, my dear husband. Glad you are back. Don't think the leak is any worse."

She casually walked to where Johnny stood and hugged him tightly. Becka walked him to the table and said, "Let's eat."

Johnny poured some warm water into the wash basin and washed his hands and face while Becka served him some hot bread and the main dish. They sat together and ate their dinner as little Johnny played by himself in his playpen.

After dinner they relaxed near the wood stove. By the light of three oil lamps, they both read a few pages from their favorite books. Little Johnny layed quietly in his playpen nearby. The couple could still hear the rain pouring down outside.

Johnny looked up from his book and mused, "What a rain storm. I wonder if my brothers made it through the mud to their friend's place? I tried to talk them out of it. So did mom."

The Franklin Family Odyssey

Becka stopped reading and commented, "Lately, what they do makes no sense. Especially Donald. He still lives with guilt about...you know what..At least that's my opinion."

"I agree, Becka. Been praying for them both. They have girl friends up the highway I guess...Sisters. Donald worries me..."

Their conversation was interrupted by a knock on the door. Johnny ran to the door and let his Dad in out of the rain.

Johnny addressed his Dad, "Is it leaking again, Dad. Do you need my help. We just finished some incredible moose stew. You want some?"

Mr. Franklin took his wet coat off and set at the table with his son and daughter-in-law. Then he answered, "I already had something to eat but I probably need your help. I'm worried about the twins. They took the old truck down to their friends on the highway. They were not happy with me when they left. And this rain...the trail

The Franklin Family Odyssey

has to be messed up. I...I just thought we could use the jeep and run down to Ferry and see if they made it off the hill without any problems."

"No problem, Dad. Isn't that right, Becka? I'll get my coat on and we can jump in the jeep and....well, check on the guys."

Becka shook her head to affirm her husbands words.

Quickly Johnny kissed his wife and little baby, put his rain gear on, and exited with his father out into the rain. Within minutes they were sloshing through the water that was everywhere. The trail was almost impassable but Mr. Franklin did a good job of not getting stuck in the first mile and a half.

The father and son proceeded through the deep forest onto the flat area near the downhill to Ferry. The mud was at least a foot thick and they could see tracks from the vehicle the twins drove down earlier in the day. They didn't see

The Franklin Family Odyssey

any signs of the other truck yet.

As they reached the downhill part of the trail, John stopped the jeep. Johnny jumped out into the mud. He could barely walk in the murky slush. The young Franklin walked tentatively but lost his balance and slid on his backside. Embarrassed, Johnny got up slowly and grabbed on to a tree limb that grew on the edge of the trail.

When he got up he could see what looked like a large object in the middle of the trail about halfway down the hill. Johnny called to his dad.

John Franklin joined his son in the muddy trail. The duo walked carefully toward a truck that was overturned in the trail. Even though it was almost dark, John thought to himself that this was his truck. As they got closer they knew for sure.

The Franklin Family Odyssey

Johnny hurried to the truck that was turned over and he checked inside. No one was in the cab so the father and son sloshed to the bottom of the hill to see if the boys made it to Devere's.

John timidly knock on Devere's cabin door. No one immediately answered. The rain continued to fall as the father and son walked around the old cabin to see if the elderly man was anywhere to be found.

John spoke to his oldest son, "Where did those boys go? Wait, isn't there another house on the other side of the river? Maybe the boys went over there."

"There's a house but I haven't seen anyone there in a while..but we can check. The boys would have to walk to their friends from here, anyway. Maybe they are up at the highway already."

John shook his head and spoke, "Yea, I guess they were determined to get to their girl friend's house. I told them to get back before 10 PM. Don't think that will happen."

"Well, should we walk up there or just head back? We need to continue to pray for the boys and their attitudes. Lord, protect my little brothers right now. Thank you, Lord."

John inserted, "Let's head back to our wives. The boys have been taught the right thing to do. I pray they use common sense."

"Dad, what about the truck? We need that truck to bring everyone down when we go get supplies this weekend?"

"Tell you what, Son, I'll make your brothers help me pull it on its wheels tomorrow. Let's hope, for their sake, that it isn't raining tomorrow and the truck will still run. Let's get the jeep home. Just a thought, maybe Devere will let me borrow the tractor one more time. We'll see."

The duo walked cautiously back up to the top of the hill and John carefully turned the jeep around without getting stuck in the mud. In half an hour they were back at John Franklin's homestead

The Franklin Family Odyssey

cabin.

The rain had subsided a bit and Johnny walked back over to his own cabin a mile away.

By the next weekend the Franklin family was ready to catch the train into Fairbanks for supplies. The big truck was put back in service, and the twins learned a good lesson in responsibility. The ladies and the baby rode in the truck with John driving while the twins were Johnny's passengers in the jeep the three miles through the mud to the Ferry railroad crossing.

A few hours later they were transported to the usual bed and breakfast in Fairbanks where they would stay until Monday or Tuesday.

Jack and Mary Jones, as was prearranged, were to meet them there later that evening. The Franklin family watched for the Jones but the they never arrived.

The Franklin Family Odyssey

Becka was very worried. She could see many scenarios for why her parents didn't meet them there.

Johnny consoled his wife, "Becka, everything is probably muddy and wet out at their place and your Dad needed to do a lot of work to get them out. They'll be here tomorrow, you'll see. No matter, God is in control, remember?"

Becka covered her face and cried for a few minutes. Johnny pulled her close and she looked up to him and smiled.

Then she said, "I know He's in control and you are right. There is probably a good explanation. We will pray they will make it tomorrow."

"Yep, we will."

Later that evening as the family got ready for bed, a guest arrived. It was Jack Jones. He brought Becka and the Franklin family the bad news that Mary had a very serious physical problem and the doctor put her in the Fairbanks hospital.

Becka was devastated and the family had a prayer vigil before they all went to bed that evening.

The Franklin Family Odyssey

Chapter ten

the fire

The Franklin family spent a month in Fairbanks while Mary Jones recuperated. It was warm and dry the whole time they were there and even though the Spring was wet, many predicted a dangerous fire season due to the unusually warm temperatures.

The young Franklin daughter visited her Mom everyday at the hospital. Becka thought to herself that Mary looked better every time she visited. The Doctors diagnosed that Mrs. Jones was almost back to normal when Johnny announced to Becka that he and his family needed to get back out to the homestead, soon.

Johnny asked Becka, "Are you going to stay here with the baby or travel back out with the rest of us? We have lots to do before winter and the experts say the fire danger is high in the Tanana and Nenana Valleys."

Becka, holding her little year and half year old, answered, "We will go back home with you. I miss the homestead. It's kind of boring here. I know there is plenty to do. I need to tend the garden and can some vegetables. Yes, we are coming aren't we, little Johnny?"

The young mother put Johnny Junior's feet on the floor and held on to his little hands. Immediately the youngster started to walk a few steps then fell to the floor.

Johnny inserted, "Becka, did you see that? He's trying to walk. Has he done that before?"

Becka quickly responded, "Oh, yes, where have you been? He walked for my Mom the other day at the hospital. He'll be running away from his uncles, soon."

The Franklin Family Odyssey

"That's cool...Except I don't know if I want him running with his uncles right now. They do some things I don't approve of and I want good influences for my growing boy."

"That's true. We need to pray for those boys. Maybe when we get back out to the homestead they will calm down and follow your Dad's rules," Becka quipped.

"I was told that they would be working really hard helping dad get ready for winter. They aren't going to like it. They want to play around all the time."

The young Franklin wife asked, "When do we leave? Soon, I hope. Mom and Dad should be living on their property within a few weeks. Mom is excited about setting up her cabin out there."

"Probably tomorrow. Is that OK?" Johnny replied.

"Sounds good to me. Let's get packed up."

The Franklin Family Odyssey

The next morning John and Alice and the rest of the Franklin clan loaded the truck with their supplies and drove to the railroad station just north of the Chena River.

By the middle of June, the Franklin family welcomed the Jones back to the homestead area. Mary seemed very strong for a person who was in the hospital for almost a month. Though happy to be back, Jack was concerned about the smoke that filled the skies and the fire threat near their homestead.

John and Johnny prepared for winter, tended huge gardens, and stock piled barrels of water just in the case of any type of fire nearby.

The father and son had heard reports that down in the little town of Healy, twenty miles south, a huge fire surrounded the village. Many fire fighters had been called in to build breaks and spread water from the river around the

The Franklin Family Odyssey

town.

Toward the end of the month, Mrs. Jones had a doctor's appointment in Fairbanks, so the Jones decided they would finish the Summer in the city due to the extreme smoke in the valley. Mary wasn't feeling very well because of the pollution.

July turned out to be one big disaster for several residents of the Nenana River Valley. Many lost cabins due to fire and thousands of acres of forest were burnt to the ground. The homesteaders above Ferry were no exception.

Johnny spoke to his Dad as they poured water around the elder Franklin's cabin, "Dad, what do you think? Are we going to be able to keep the fires away from us. I keep thinking about my dream and the fire was a major part the terror I can still see."

"One thing we need to do is to be of

good courage. That's straight from God's word. I know your dream could be prophetic but it may not be either. Let's just be prepared for anything that happens. You protect your family. If you need to leave, go ahead. I'm staying here through thick or thin."

Johnny smiled broadly and spoke, "I knew you would say that. I'm not leaving and I think I can speak for my wife, as well. We will be OK because we are prepared. My Dad taught me that a long time ago."

Dad and son both laughed as they rolled a loaded barrel of water closer to John Franklin's cabin.

Both families settle for the evening in their own homes with confidence the fires would not get much closer. Johnny still wanted to do one more checking outside his small cabin so he went out into the twilight of an Alaskan Summer. The first thing he noticed is that there was a south wind that had began to blow softly through the trees. This was a change from a few hours earlier. There was no wind at all.

As Johnny was always taught, any wind is not good during fire seasons. The young homesteader whispered a prayer and then went back into his cabin for the evening.

Later that night, Johnny was awakened by a whimper coming from an almost two year old child. As he got up, the young father could smell the strong smell of smoke in the house. He quickly grabbed his son and woke his wife."

"Becka, let's get out of here. There is a fire nearby. Maybe even our cabin. Let's go."

The young mother shook herself awake and dressed quickly. The Young Franklins and their baby hurried out the front door. As Johnny ran with little

The Franklin Family Odyssey

Johnny, he quickly turned and spotted a huge flame a few feet behind their house. He watched as it jumped onto the roof of the log structure.

Becka screamed, "Our house, Johnny, let's get to your parents quickly. We need to get off this mountain or at least a few miles away."

Johnny gave the baby to Becka and told her to get to his parent's cabin as fast as she could. He stayed behind to see what he could do. For the next few minutes Johnny threw buckets of water from his barrels, up toward the roof and on the cabin.

Hopelessly the young homesteader did what he could to save his house. A half hour later John arrived to check on his son in his attempt to save the cabin.

By the time the elder Franklin arrived, most of the cabin roof was on fire and the area behind the house was fully a

The Franklin Family Odyssey

blazed. John helped scatter water for a while until the barrels ran dry.

The elder Franklin watched as Johnny desperately pounded at the fire with an old rug. Mr. Franklin through his hands in the air.

He then pulled Johnny away from his house and said carefully, "Johnny, it's no use. It's gone. Let's try to keep it from moving any other direction right now. It's a good thing Jack brushed quite a ways around this cabin, accept for the back. That's a lesson for us from here on."

"But, Dad, all off our stuff. Becka's rocking chair and the crib...and a thousand other things."

John again pulled his son away from the fire and looked into his disappointed eyes. Then he said, "Yes, son, they are just things. That's all they are. We can replace your rocker and your clothes, but I can't replace you. You and your beautiful wife

The Franklin Family Odyssey

and baby are safe and alive."

Johnny fell to the ground and stuck his head between his legs. Then he looked heavenward and began, "Thank you, my dear Lord, for saving us, my wife, my baby and me. Thank you for waking me before the cabin caught on fire."

The young father began to weep profusely. His dad knelt down and hugged him from behind and prayed, "Comfort my son, dear Father. Though his dream has come true You saved him for another adventure. Give him strength today. Give Becka endurance. Thank you again for saving them from them inferno. Thank you."

As John finished his pray, Becka walked up to her husband who was still knelt on the ground. She prayed, "You are a glorious God. Thank you for my brave husband who did his best to save our house. Thank you for saving us. What a God."

Chapter eleven
the miracle

With little Johnny walking around in the way, Johnny and Becka prepared the inside of their new cabin given to them by the elder Jones. A few days earlier Johnny and his Dad did the best they could to salvage some of the young Franklin's belongings from the burnt cabin.

John was able to find a Bible that was only singed by the fire. Johnny pulled Becka's rocking chair out of the rubble and contemplated how he could repair it.

The young couple was still grieving over losing their cabin and many other things, but they were relieved that the whole family was safe and that there was a home to move in to.

The Franklin Family Odyssey

Earlier in the week the elder Franklins purchased several changes of clothes for Becka, Johnny and little Johnny since they had lost most of their belongings in the fire just two weeks before. Becka's parents also shopped for their daughter, grandchild and son-in-law. Jack, Becka's father, purchased a new bed for the couple and in addition, a large sofa for their living area.

At the same time the entire Franklin family was bemoaning the fact that the Franklin twins were prepared to leave home and move into Fairbanks. Denny and Donald both were promised work in the city and they were excited about being on their own. The entire family prayed the best for the twins, but each family member had some doubts due to their lack of responsibility in the past.

John helped the boys pack the truck as they got ready to drive down to Ferry and take the train north to Fairbanks. The sad father reluctantly drove Donald and

The Franklin Family Odyssey

Denny the three miles to the tracks. To himself, he recalled many twin memories and he prayed for their future. John even wondered if he'd ever see them again with the attitude they personified.

The disappointed father said his goodbyes to his two sons as they boarded the train. Again John silently prayed for Denny and Donald. Before they left, the elder Franklin arranged to visit them in a few weeks up in Fairbanks. They agreed so John felt a sense of relief.

The train left and John looked into the heavens on his walk back to his truck. The elderly Devere, who lived near the tracks, called to him. "Hey, neighbor, boys heading to town?"

Franklin quickly turned around and walked back toward Devere. Then he answered his friend, "Yea, kind of sad but I taught them how to make it on their own. I pray I did a good job."

The Franklin Family Odyssey

"I'm sure you did, John. Been watching you all these years. You have taught them well. I wish I could say I did the same. Haven't heard from my boys in years. Sometimes I feel sad about it but.."

John inserted, "I'm not that sure about my boys. Right now they are upset with me. I don't have lots of money and they thought they were deserving of some kind of compensation from me. They have expensive girl friends, I take it."

"I wouldn't worry. You going to visit them in town, soon?"

"That's the plan. We'll see. I know where they're staying for now. Nice talking to you, Devere. Got to get back up and help my older son setting up his new cabin. He lost almost everything in the fire. You do know he dreamed about this fire for years? I don't think he wanted it to actually happen but it did."

"I think Johnny might have mention

his dream to me a year ago but...Dreams are dreams. They don't come true do they?"

"I believe dreaming is very important and they can come to pass, but that's God's business not ours. The good book says 'All things work together for the good to them called according to His purpose.'"

"Wow, is that so. Well, John, I got to run myself. Playing cards later with some friends from Healy. Talk to you later."

John shook Devere's hand and turned again to walk to his truck. A light rain started to fall as the elder Franklin got back in his truck. A half hour later he was home. He then walked the two miles to Johnny's new cabin to assist his son and daughter-in-law.

A month later John and Alice along with their grandchild, Johnny and Becka traveled the train into Fairbanks. Their missions were to buy supplies, to visit

The Franklin Family Odyssey

with the twins and to check on the Jones, north of the city.

Arranged in advance, Jack Jones met the family at the train and drove them out to their new house in the Chena Flats. As they traveled toward the Jones' new residence, the Franklins noticed the many burnt out areas and destroyed houses that were blazed earlier in the Summer. Jack told his passengers that the fires didn't even come close to their new house.

Becka asked her Dad, "How's mom doing. We've been praying for her."

"It was touch and go for a while there after we left the homestead in June. Basically we were stuck in the house for weeks, but....Wait, till you see her. I'll let her tell you how she is when we get to the house."

As the vehicle pulled into the driveway, Mary Jones watched for the truck. She was out on the porch waiting

The Franklin Family Odyssey

for her guest. The Franklin family would be the very first visitors to their beautiful new house and property.

Jack was anxious to show John and Johnny his garden and small corral he built for a few cows he planned to purchase soon. He also bragged about the log fence he had built around the whole ten acres.

While the men followed Jack around, Mrs. Jones escorted Alice and Becka into her fancy kitchen which had a new gas stove that she just had shipped from the lower forty-eight. In the living room Mary pointed out the large rock fire place with a black bear rug lying in front of the hearth.

When the gentlemen came in from the outside, Jack led the men into his large garage and work room that was located through a door on one side of the living area.

Following the grand tour, both

The Franklin Family Odyssey

families went into the dining area where the table was prepared with lunch for everyone.

After everyone ate their full, it was getting late in the afternoon, and John told his host and hostess that he and his family needed to get to the bed and breakfast. The Jones couple tried to talk the Franklin's into staying the night with them. Johnny and Becka were excited about the idea but John and Alice had plans to go back into town to check on the twins.

Jack inserted, "You two could see the twins tomorrow, couldn't you? We have plenty of room."

John whispered in his wife's ear and then he replied, "I guess that would be OK. I told the boys we would see them today, but who knows if I'll be able to see them anyway. They could be working. I haven't heard from either one of them since they left home."

The Franklin Family Odyssey

Mary timidly spoke, "I've been looking forward to have you all stay at least one night with us. My grandson and his parents have a room just for them, and we built a guest room for our best friends, the Franklins. "

Alice quickly responded, "Oh, we so appreciate you and Jack all these years. God has blessed us with you folks as friends for a long time. This beautiful place is like having a honeymoon vacation all over again."

John laughed and inserted, "She said that because we never had a honeymoon."

They all laughed as Mary led Alice to the guest room. The male Franklins went out to the truck to get their bags and bring them inside.

The next morning after a good nights sleep in unfamiliar beds, the Franklins got up early and Mary fixed them all a good breakfast of ham and eggs with some

The Franklin Family Odyssey

freshly squeezed orange juice.

Jack Jones drove the Franklins to the bed and breakfast and John immediately asked at the front desk if Donald and Denny Franklin were still checked in. He was told the twins hadn't been staying there for two weeks.

After checking in themselves, John and Johnny decided they would walk around town to ask about the missing teens.

The father and son hiked for two hours asking several people if they knew Donald and Denny. They searched but with no sign of the twins.

Giving up for the evening, the duo started back toward the bed and breakfast. The wind was blowing in Johnny's face rather heavily when the young man stopped abruptly in the middle of a block just around the corner from the B and B. He pointed toward the front of a little bar and restaurant.

Johnny spoke, "Dad, I think.. That looks Denny. Let's go!"

Johnny led the way and John followed him tentatively. Johnny called out, "Denny, Denny."

A young man fifty feet away turned around and stared at John and Johnny as they grew nearer.

The young man answered, "Are you looking for Denny Franklin?"

Johnny walked up to the stranger who wasn't his brother and spoke, "Oh, thought you my brother from a distance. Do you know my brother, Denny?"

"Yes, we worked together this morning at the boat docks on the Chena River. My name is Cecil, Cecil Reavers. I work there just in the Summer, part time."

The Franklin Family Odyssey

John pushed past Johnny and asked Cecil, "Have seen him since you worked with him? Where does he live?"

"Sir, I don't know where he lives but I heard he was with his brother. I guess a twin brother."

Johnny inserted, "That's Donald. We are looking for them both. They aren't really missing. We knew they were here but we came to see them at the bed and breakfast around the corner. They told us they haven't been there in two weeks."

Cecil continued, "He's...Denny has only worked where I work for a short time. He didn't tell me where he lived. But wait a girl in this bar knows Denny. Let me run in here and ask her about Denny. Be right back."

Cecil scampered through the door of the bar. Five minutes later he came back out and spoke, "She ....I guess she lives with him in a room on the next block in a

The Franklin Family Odyssey

boarding house. Just directly behind us here. She said number five was the room. He's probably there. She knew nothing of his brother."

John again spoke, "Thanks for the help, young man. You have been very helpful."

Johnny repeated the sentiment.

The father and son duo walked around the block and found the boarding house in the middle of the block. They quietly walked up the narrow, dark stair well and turned right into the dimly lit hallway that led to the rooms. John walked deliberately down to room five with Johnny followed him. The elder Franklin knocked on the door.

Someone called from the room, "Who is it. Is that you Cecil? I'll be right out."

Denny opened the door and found his dad and older brother standing in the doorway. With his mouth wide open he tried to speak, "Ohhhhhh, Dad and Johnny, what are you two doing here? I was…..My friend was to come up and see me."

John spoke softly, "Is his name Cecil? We just met him around the block. He sent us here a few minutes ago."

Johnny quickly inserted, "Yea, he lied at first saying he didn't know where you lived. This is your type of friends now days?"

Denny started to say something and immediately stopped.

John again spoke, "We made an arrangement with you two boys to come and visit you. But you haven't been at the bed and breakfast for a couple of weeks. I thought I paid a month in advance for you guys."

"I...I don't know what to say, Dad. I have no idea where Donald is. We both lost our jobs a few weeks ago. I just got another one down at the river."

Johnny answered, "Yea, we were told that you work with Cecil. At least that was the truth."

John had a worried look on his face and then he asked, "I'm concerned. Where is Donald?"

Denny shook his head and spoke, "He didn't tell me where he was going but....he was with his girl..somewhere north of here."

John turned around to walk away and Johnny followed him, then the elder son asked, "Dad, are you alright. We will find him. We found Denny didn't we?"

Turning back to his older son he said, "I know we will. Let's go tell your mother. Denny, are you going to come and see your mom before we go back to the

The Franklin Family Odyssey

homestead? We leave day after tomorrow."

Denny frowned and answered, "Sure, we...I will be there. You can count on it."

John and Johnny solemnly and quietly walked back to the bed a breakfast a few blocks away. John was not looking forward to telling Alice about the twins and what they were doing.

A day and a half later the Franklins were again to be picked up by Jack and Mary. The Jones offered to transport the family to the train depot at about noon.

Just shortly before the Jones' arrival, Johnny casually peaked around the corner as if he was waiting or looking for someone.

John noticed his older son's actions and asked, "Looking for Denny again, son. You certainly are a very good older brother."

The Franklin Family Odyssey

Johnny stopped and turned around, "Yea, I believed him. Wait, Dad, here he comes. He's carrying a satchel. Maybe he's coming home with us."

"Hey, Johnny, you lookin for me? Sorry it took me so long. I remember the many talks you and I and Dad have had over these seventeen years. You have room for a strangler?"

John went straight to his twin son and gave him a great big hug. Then he spoke, "Son, my son, the one who was gone is now found. Let's have a party."

Denny pushed his dad away for a moment and then began, "But, Dad, I didn't find Donald. I've been looking all over town, but no luck."

Denny continued with a distraught look on his face, "I don't have any friends with a vehicle to travel up north. Can I help you and Johnny find him after we get home? You are going to look for him,

The Franklin Family Odyssey

aren't you?"

John replied, "We will find him, I'm sure. God is in control and he loves Donald and he loves you."

A few hours later the Franklin family arrived at the homestead. Johnny walked Becka and the baby to the cabin and then returned for their supplies and suitcases.

On his return he walked up to his Dad and Denny as they talked. Denny said, "Dad, I...I know I screwed up by running off with Donald, but would you consider giving me a few acres on the north side of the homestead so I can build my own cabin." Denny watch as Johnny approached and continued, "And...., big brother can you and Dad help me?"

"Sure enough, Denny. I'll always be there for you and Donald just like in the old days."

The Franklin Family Odyssey

Denny addressed his Dad, "When will we go up north to look for Donald. I have some ideas where we might find him. I hope soon..I miss him."

The elder Franklin responded, "Soon, son, soon. Won't we Johnny?"

The Franklin Family Odyssey

Books from David Erickson

The Northern Force Series book one and two

Amazon.com and Kindle

The Franklin Family Odyssey

The Northern Force book thee and four

Amazon.com and Kindle

The Franklin Family Odyssey

Other books from David Erickson

The Northern Force Book 5

Amazon.com and Kindle

The Franklin Family Odyssey

www.ingramcontent.com/pod-product-compliance
Lightning Source LLC
Chambersburg PA
CBHW072347090226
39424CB00009B/276